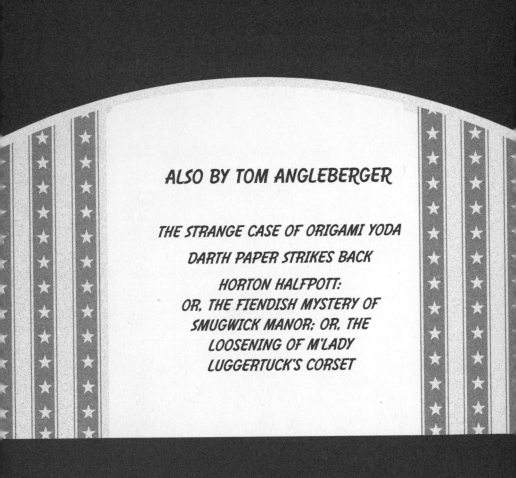

ALSO BY TOM ANGLEBERGER

THE STRANGE CASE OF ORIGAMI YODA

DARTH PAPER STRIKES BACK

HORTON HALFPOTT:
OR, THE FIENDISH MYSTERY OF
SMUGWICK MANOR; OR, THE
LOOSENING OF M'LADY
LUGGERTUCK'S CORSET

AMULET BOOKS ★ NEW YORK

FAKE MUSTACHE

OR, HOW JODIE O'RODEO AND HER WONDER HORSE (AND SOME NERDY KID) SAVED THE U.S PRESIDENTIAL ELECTION FROM A MAD GENIUS CRIMINAL MASTERMIND

★ ★ ★ ★ ★ ★ ★ ★ ★ ★ ★ ★

TOM ANGLEBERGER
ILLUSTRATED BY JEN WANG

THE LIBRARY OF CONGRESS HAS CATALOGUED THE HARDCOVER EDITION OF THIS BOOK AS FOLLOWS:

ANGLEBERGER, TOM.
FAKE MUSTACHE : HOW JODIE O'RODEO AND HER WONDER HORSE (AND SOME NERDY GUY) SAVED THE U.S. PRESIDENTIAL ELECTION FROM A MAD GENIUS CRIMINAL MASTERMIND / BY TOM ANGLEBERGER.
P. CM.
ISBN 978-1-4197-0194-8 (HARDBACK)
[1. CRIMINALS—FICTION. 2. MUSTACHES—FICTION. 3. DISGUISE—FICTION. 4. HYPNOTISM—FICTION. 5. POLITICS, PRACTICAL—FICTION. 6. HUMOROUS STORIES.] I. TITLE.
PZ7.A585FAK 2012
[FIC]—DC23
2012000556

PAPERBACK ISBN: 978-1-4197-0698-1

TEXT COPYRIGHT © 2012 TOM ANGLEBERGER
ILLUSTRATIONS COPYRIGHT © 2012 JEN WANG
BOOK DESIGN BY MEAGAN BENNETT

PRINTED AND BOUND IN THE U.S.A.

10 9 8 7 6 5 4 3 2 1

AMULET BOOKS ARE AVAILABLE AT SPECIAL DISCOUNTS WHEN PURCHASED IN QUANTITY FOR PREMIUMS AND PROMOTIONS AS WELL AS FUNDRAISING OR EDUCATIONAL USE. SPECIAL EDITIONS CAN ALSO BE CREATED TO SPECIFICATION. FOR DETAILS, CONTACT SPECIALSALES@ABRAMSBOOKS.COM OR THE ADDRESS BELOW.

ABRAMS
THE ART OF BOOKS SINCE 1949
115 WEST 18TH STREET
NEW YORK, NY 10011
WWW.ABRAMSBOOKS.COM

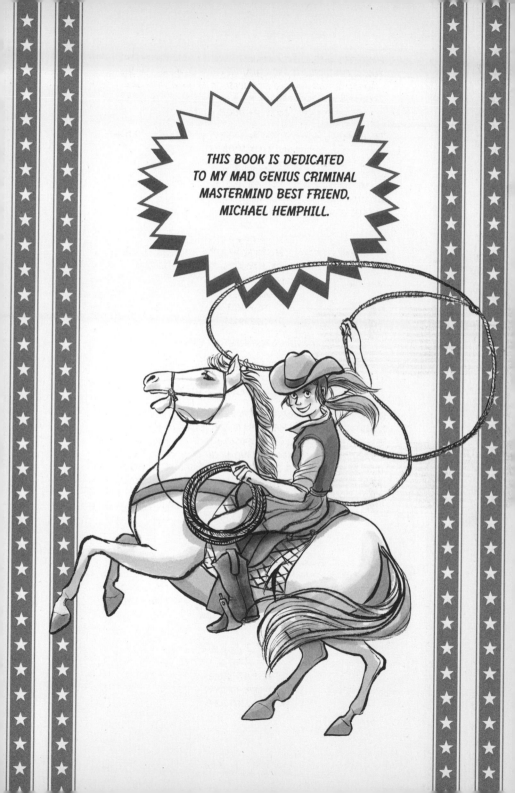

PART I

You may remember seeing me on TV when Jodie O'Rodeo saved the world. I was that nerdy guy in the background that nobody could figure out what he was doing there. But nobody really cared because Jodie O'Rodeo had just saved the world. Remember?

Well, that was me, Lenny Flem Jr., and believe it or not, I saved the world too. Me and Jodie saved the world together. And this is the story of how we did it.

Don't worry, we'll get to Jodie's part soon. But don't skip ahead, because if you do, you won't have any idea what she's talking about.

See, it all started with me and my friend Casper going to Sven's Fair Price Store in downtown Hairsprinkle.

Don't ever buy a fake mustache at Sven's Fair Price Store.

Sven's Fair Price Store is an awesome place, and I recommend it if you want to buy fake tattoos, fake noses, fake thumbs, fake eyelashes, fake tuxedo shirts, fake books that have secret compartments, fake laughter machines, fake fog makers, fake feet, fake teeth that you wind up, fake teeth that you stick in your mouth, fake gum that snaps people's fingers, fake dog poop, or fake people poop.

But the fake mustaches are just *too* good. They're made out of real human mustache hair. Apparently, there are men in Belgium who grow their mustaches for a year, then cut them off and sell them to the Heidelberg Novelty Company.

This makes the fake mustaches really expensive. But they're worth it . . . if you really want a good fake mustache—which you don't! It'll only lead to trouble. That's what I'm trying to tell you.

If you buy one, you get this stuff called "spirit gum" for free. That's what you use to stick the mustache to your face. It really works and it makes the mustache look really, really real.

I didn't buy one. My friend Casper Bengue bought one. I got this sticky hand on the end of a sticky stretchy rubber kind of thing. It's called the Super-Sticky Hand. You can flick it a long way and it'll stick to whatever it lands on—like a penny, maybe—and then the rubber band part will zip it back to you . . . with the penny. The hand comes in a little plastic egg so that the stickiness doesn't wear off in your pocket.

It might seem like a stupid thing to choose, but maybe it was my destiny rather than just a dumb idea. Either way, it's a good thing I got it because otherwise . . . well, I'm not sure what would have happened, but it would have been bad in a huge, earthshaking, TV-news-special-report kind of way.

Actually, things turned out bad in a huge, earthshaking, TV-news-special-report kind of way anyway. But that wasn't because of the sticky hand. That was because of the fake mustache.

It was Casper who wanted to buy the best, most expensive fake mustache at Sven's.

"Look at this, Lenny," he said to me at his birthday party. (I was the only one who came.) "My nana Nookums gave me four hundred dollars."

Casper's parents are hippies who don't believe in buying anything unnecessary, but every once in a while his rich grandmother gives him money and makes him promise to buy something as unnecessary as possible. That's why Casper's family has a doorbell that says welcome in the voices of two hundred different country-and-western stars, but they don't have regular stuff that every other family has—like a TV.

"Nana Nookums wants me to buy a PlayStation."

"Awesome," I said. "But how can you play a PlayStation without a TV?"

"Precisely," said Casper. "It's absolutely pointless for me to follow my nana Nookums's orders. So I think that means I can ethically spend the money any way I want to."

"Really? Are you going to buy a TV?"

"Of course not. I'm going to buy a fake mustache."

"What? A four-hundred-dollar fake mustache?"

"No, the one I've had my eye on—the Heidelberg Handlebar Number Seven—is $129.99 at Sven's Fair Price Store. I'm going to use the rest of the money to get a first-class man-about-town suit."

"Why do you need a first-class man-about-town suit? You're not a man-about-town."

"I'm not now, but that's only because I don't have the suit yet. Anyway, you want to come with me downtown? I'm going right now."

"Sure," I said.

I've heard that people in other towns say Hairsprinkle is a very strange place. Maybe because nothing ever changes here. Back like a hundred years ago, lots of towns had trolley cars that went right down the middle of the street on tracks, just like little trains.

Eventually, people got their own cars and didn't want trolley cars anymore and got tired of bumping over the trolley tracks all the time. So all these towns paved over the tracks and sold the trolleys for scrap.

But not Hairsprinkle. Hairsprinkle still has its trolleys, and you can still ride them for ten cents. The people in Hairsprinkle won't elect anyone to be mayor unless he or she promises to never change a thing. My dad, Lenny Flem Sr., says that it costs a ton of money to keep the trolleys running and the ten-cent fare doesn't even begin to pay for it, and that's why his taxes are so high and he's sick of it.

But I'm not sick of it. I love riding the trolleys. One

of them goes down Hair Avenue, just two blocks down Sprinkle Street from where me and Casper live.

So it's not a big deal to tell our parents we're going downtown, walk two blocks, pay ten cents, and ride right into the city. We do it all the time. And Casper and I have spent a lot of time downtown at Sven's Fair Price Store and the Hairsprinkle Hot Dog and other places.

But I had never bothered to go into Chauncey's Big & Small, Short & Tall before. That's the first place Casper wanted to go that fateful day.

Are you boys selling candy bars for your *GottDangled* school? No more candy bars! Get the *Helchfitz* out of here!"

I was ready to get the *Helchfitz* out of the store, but Casper didn't budge.

"Don't worry," he whispered. "When you've got four hundred dollars to spend, you get treated differently."

"Are you Chauncey?" he asked the angry man.

"No!"

"Where is Chauncey?"

"Dead!"

"Oh, I'm sorry," said Casper.

"He died in 1908. I'm his brother, Red."

If Chauncey had died over a hundred years ago, I didn't have any idea how old Red was. Nor was there anything red about him. But it didn't seem smart to ask personal questions.

"I'd like a suit," said Casper.

"Go to the *GottDangled* Walmart like everybody else. We don't have a kids' section!"

"I don't want a kids' suit. Kids' suits make you look stupid. I want a man-about-town suit for a short man-about-town. And I've got cash."

Red pulled out a ribbon and lunged at Casper. I thought he was attacking him. But Casper stood perfectly still while Red held the ribbon around his stomach, across his shoulders, from his armpit to his wrist, from his knee to his ankle, from his nose to his belly button, and on and on. He never wrote anything down and he didn't seem to be paying attention to the measurements he was taking, because he was rattling off questions like a bag of microwave popcorn. Amazingly, Casper answered every question in about a microsecond.

Double- or single-breasted?

Single.

Worsted?

Yes.

Belt or suspenders?

Suspenders.

Button fly or zipper?

Button.

Pinstripe or herringbone?

Herringbone.

I got bored and looked around. Mostly it was just racks and racks of suits, some really, really small and some really, really, really big. I've never seen anyone in Hairsprinkle big enough to fit into some of those things.

On a table I saw a stack of fuzzy gray hats. But then I wondered if they were really gray and fuzzy or if they were covered by a thick coat of dust.

I reached out a finger.

It was dust.

"Leave those hats alone, you *FarDobbled* Candy-Bar-Selling Punkler!" screamed Red.

I turned around quick and saw Red and Casper rolling their eyes at me!

"I've got just what you need, sir," Red said to Casper. "The Statesman Deluxe by Porco Risotto Brothers of Milan. It won't even need tailoring. A perfect fit."

He grabbed the closest suit off the closest rack.

"Just $249.99. Comes with a free cravat."

I went over to see it. It was nice, but . . .

"That's a lot of money," I whispered to Casper.

"It's perfect," said Casper. "Even with tax, I'll still have just enough left to buy the Heidelberg Handlebar Number Seven."

And so he bought the suit.

Red grabbed the money and petted it and cooed at it while Casper put the suit on. Then Red gave Casper a paper bag for his old clothes and handed him the cravat, which is apparently sort of like a tie. Casper told me he didn't really want it and took it only because it was free.

"Come back anytime!" shouted Red. "Well, not both of you! Not the little Parboiled Snert, but the other one!"

Then Casper and I walked out of the store.

"Wow, look at that short man-about-town!" exclaimed a passerby.

"I wonder why he's hanging around with that nerdy kid," said another.

I had to admit it, Casper did look a little bit more like a short man-about-town than a slightly tall nerdy seventh grader, while I still looked like a slightly short nerdy seventh grader. Maybe I should have bought a dusty hat.

*H*ey, let's stop at Hairsprinkle Hot Dog next," I said as we walked up the street.

"No thanks," said Casper. "I don't want to get mustard on my suit."

"Can we at least stop in for a drink? I'm dying. I think I inhaled a pound of dust back at Chauncey's."

Casper glared at me. "Look, I'm not going anywhere near that grease pit with this suit on."

"Well, if you're so worried about it, why don't you put your regular clothes back on?"

"I have my reasons."

"And why are you holding your hand over your face?"

"There are people who shouldn't see me without the mustache."

I looked around. It looked like just the usual Hairsprinkle kind of people, except there did seem to be more than the usual number of strolling accordion players.

"Look," he said, "go have a hot dog if you want, but I'm going to Sven's."

"All right, all right, I'm coming."

I don't think the stuff in Sven's Fair Price Store changes very often, but there's so much of it that you can only see a tiny bit at a time. So every time you go in there, you see something new. Like the sticky hand thing I told you about. I had never seen those before, so I decided to get one.

Since it was almost Halloween, I noticed there *were* more costumes than usual. But I didn't want a costume, so I looked in the stationery aisle.

That's where I found a Wet Pets pen. It was a ball-point pen and the top end was made of clear plastic. Inside, there was grungy water and some flecks that seemed to be swimming around. It came with a little book called *Care and Feeding of Your Water Hogs*.

It was $7.99, and I was sort of thinking about getting one when Casper came over.

"They've raised the price on the Heidelberg Handlebar Number Seven!" he moaned. "How much money have you got?"

I ripped open the Velcro on my wallet. I had a ten-dollar bill and a one-dollar bill.

"Let me have the ten dollars!" Casper begged. He

seemed pretty upset, but I didn't really want to give him ten bucks.

"C'mon, it's my birthday," he said.

"But I already gave you a present," I said.

"It was junk," said Casper.

I couldn't argue with that. About five years ago, my mother bought a bunch of Famous Presidents of History action figures at Sultan's Salvage Store. Any time I get invited to a birthday party, she makes me give one as a present. Nobody wants them, and that may be one reason I rarely get invited to birthday parties anymore.

"No offense, but who wants a Herbert Hoover action figure?" sneered Casper. "You owe me a real present."

"All right, fine," I said, and gave him the ten bucks.

This, of course, was a terrible, terrible mistake. A mistake that would change the course of history. But please, *please* believe me that if I had known what that ten dollars would do, I never would have given it to Casper. Never.

Chapter
5

FAKE MUSTACHE

The Heidelberg Handlebar Number Seven was in a glass case. The cashier told us he wasn't permitted to open the case, so he went to get the manager, who turned out to be a very, very angry-looking lady wearing a name tag that said HI, MY NAME IS SVEN!

She was text-messaging someone with her cell phone and didn't even look up at us.

"I don't have time to fool around with the mustaches," she bellowed. "Just get one of the cheap ones from the pile." She gestured to a stack of hundreds and hundreds of shrink-wrapped fake mustaches.

They were marked $2.99 and looked like they had been sitting there since before Sven was born.

"I'm interested in the Heidelberg Handlebar Number Seven," said Casper.

For the first time, Sven glanced up. She looked very closely at Casper. Her eyes went up and down, noting the sharp creases in his pants . . . the herringbone pattern in his suit coat . . . the way his suspenders hooked on to his pants with buttons, not metal clamps.

"I beg your pardon, sir," she said, tossing her cell phone on the counter and pulling a tangled mass of key chains from her pocket. She rummaged through the mess until she found what seemed to be the only key.

"See?" whispered Casper. "The suit worked."

Sven unlocked the cabinet and punched in a code on a little keypad to disable the alarm. There was a whooshing sound as the door opened.

Using a long pair of tweezers, she picked up the mustache and then placed it into a felt-lined box, which she snapped shut when she was done.

The cashier started to ring up the purchase on the cash register, but Sven put out a hand to stop him. "One formality. The Heidelberg Novelty Company requires me to ask the purpose of your purchase."

"Our school is putting on a musical adaptation of *The Hoboken Chicken Emergency*," Casper replied, "and I've been chosen to play the mayor."

This was a complete and total lie.

"Impressive," said Sven, raising one side of the thick eyebrow that grew across her forehead. "That is a role that takes real gravitas. The mustache will serve you well . . . Here, please take a complimentary year's

supply of spirit gum. It will keep the mustache on your lip through thick and thin."

"Thank you, Sven," Casper said gravely as she handed him a ziplock bag containing a wad of goo.

"Proceed with the sale," Sven instructed the cashier.

When Casper had paid, both Sven and the cashier looked at me expectantly.

"I just want this," I said, and put the little egg with the sticky hand on the counter.

Sven wrinkled her nose in disgust.

The cashier, sneering, hit a few buttons on the cash register and said, "That'll be four fifty."

"But the sign said ninety-nine cents," I said.

"JUST TAKE IT AND GET OUT OF HERE, YOU PATHETIC, SLIGHTLY SHORT, NERDY SEVENTH GRADER!" bellowed Sven.

C asper and I got back on the trolley and went home. "Happy birthday," I said, just to be polite. Frankly, I was annoyed by everything that had happened. I had lost ten bucks, been treated like a child twice, and didn't even get a Hairsprinkle hot dog.

Casper looked me in the eye. He shook my hand and patted me on the shoulder. And then he said, "Goodbye, Lenny. Wherever fate leads us tomorrow, please remember that we have walked far in friendship."

"Uh . . . yeah . . . real far. Right. Um . . . see you," I said, with no idea why he was making such a big deal about stuff.

I went home to supper. We eat supper in front of the TV and we vote on what we want to watch. My mom, dad, and I all vote for different things. My sisters both always vote for *The Jodie O'Rodeo Showdeo*. So they win every time.

To tell you the truth, I'm too embarrassed to vote for it, but I don't really mind watching it. I mean, the plots are stupid—mostly about going to the mall—and now they're all reruns because the show was canceled. Worst of all, the singing is annoying and lip-synched. But Jodie O'Rodeo, the preteen cowgirl queen, is the coolest girl I've ever seen. She rides a horse and does rope tricks and is pretty cute.

It goes like this . . .

SCENE: JODIE'S BEDROOM

We see Jodie sleeping in a tangle of sheets, blankets, and stuffed animals.

A cell phone rings.

Without getting up, Jodie reaches for it, but picks up a cowgirl boot instead.

> JODIE
> *speaking into the boot*
> Hello?

[LAUGH TRACK]

She drops boot and picks up cell phone.

                    JODIE
          Hello?

Split screen showing Jodie and her best
friend, Kat.

                    KAT
          Oh. My. Gosh! Jodie, what are you
          doing?

                    JODIE
          Sleeping!

[LAUGH TRACK]

                    KAT
          Why aren't you at the mall!!

                    JODIE
          Didn't I tell you? I'm grounded!

                    KAT
          What for?

                    JODIE
        Remember when I said my dad
        wouldn't mind if I borrowed his
        credit card to get those boots with
        the red, white, and blue fringe?

                    KAT
        Yeah. So?

                    JODIE
        He minded!

[LAUGH TRACK]

                    JODIE
        Now, if you'll excuse me, I'm asleep!

                    KAT
        OK, fine, Lala, I just thought
        you might want to know what your
        boyfriend is doing . . . Answer:
        Buying Shayla an Orange Julius!

Jodie sits straight up in bed, sending her
stuffed animals flying.

JODIE

Now I'm awake!

[LAUGH TRACK]

JODIE

I'll be right there!

KAT

I thought you were grounded?

JODIE

Well, it's like Ol' Gramps says,
"Sometimes it's better to break
a rule . . . than to break your
heart!"

EXTERIOR SHOT OF JODIE'S HOUSE

Second-story window opens. Jodie sticks
head out window.

JODIE

"Hey-YO-yo-te-do, Soymilk!"

Soymilk the Wonder Horse gallops past
house just as Jodie jumps from window and
lands perfectly on Soymilk's back.

[CUE: MUSIC MONTAGE. Shots of Soymilk
galloping across town, weaving in and out of
traffic, jumping fences while Jodie rides,
yodels, and sings her new single, "You're
Breakin' My Rule About Breakin' My Heart."]

This was the episode about someone trying to rob
the Orange Julius stand at the mall, so Jodie O'Rodeo
had to ride her horse down the escalator and lasso the
robbers. Then she yodeled, and then her boyfriend gave
her the Orange Julius he had bought for Shayla, who
accidentally stepped in horse poo.

I've seen the episode so many times, I think I've
learned how to yodel just by watching it, but I haven't
figured out how they did the horse-on-the-escalator
trick.

After supper, I practiced using my new sticky hand.
It turned out to be pretty hard to pick up anything with
it, even a penny that was just a few feet away. I was just
starting to get the hang of it when Dad told me I was
driving him crazy and made me go to bed.

*T*he next morning when I went into the kitchen, my mom and dad were watching the *Good Morning Hairsprinkle* show. They watch it every morning, even though it's the same people shouting at each other or sharing cooking tips. But this morning there was actual news.

"Look, Lenny Junior! Someone robbed the First Bank of Hairsprinkle!" my dad said. Since he's Lenny Senior, he always calls me Lenny Junior. "This is the national news! Hairsprinkle is actually on the national news!"

"Look, Puddingcup, that's our bank! I was just there last week," said my mom. When I was a baby, I liked pudding, so she still calls me Puddingcup. It's better than what she calls my sisters. "Wow, I'm lucky to be alive! I wonder if NewsAttack wants to interview me?"

"Look," said my dad, "it's Giorgio 'Jim' McPunklett, the famous CNT NewsAttack anchor. He's right here in—"

"This is Giorgio 'Jim' McPunklett, the famous CNT NewsAttack anchor, reporting live from Hairsprinkle, where the first-ever billion-dollar bank robbery was carried out in the wee hours of the morning by a gang of strolling accordion players. Police have arrested several members of the gang—all of whom claim to have no idea what is going on—but haven't found the missing money or the ringleader. The bank's security cameras caught the robbery on film, and, as you can see, the ringleader appears to be a short, well-dressed man-about-town sporting a spectacular handlebar mustache."

*L*ater, at school, I ran into Casper in the hall.

"Hey, Lenny, I'm sorry about yesterday."

"Which part?" I asked.

"The part where I complained about your birthday present and made you give me ten dollars. Herbert Hoover is actually a great action figure. I want to give you your money back."

He handed me a bill.

"Uh, Casper, this is a ten-thousand-dollar bill."

"Whoopsie!" he said, taking it back. He rooted around in his backpack for a minute, then pulled out a ten.

I just looked at it. Finally, I said, "Casper, did you rob that bank last night?"

"What bank?"

"The bank downtown that got robbed!"

"Really? There was a bank robbery?"

"Yeah, really. It's all over the news. The national news!"

"Huh, well, you know, we don't have a TV, so I didn't see the news."

The homeroom bell rang.

"Tell me about it at lunch," said Casper, and he pushed the ten-dollar bill into my hand and headed down the hall.

I looked at the bill. It was stiff and crisp . . . like a bill that had just come fresh from the bank.

I realized that Casper had never answered my question.

As it turned out, I didn't see Casper at lunch. They closed school early because of the manhunt for the criminal mastermind of the bank robbery. Even though nobody had been hurt in the bank robbery, the FBI was worried that the leader of the gang might be dangerous. He had instantly become the second-most wanted criminal in the United States, behind that lady who stole the president's underpants last year.

So the FBI agents and the police and the K-9 squad were searching all over Hairsprinkle. My dad wouldn't let me out of the house to go see Casper. I tried texting him, but he didn't write back.

I just couldn't figure it out. Could Casper *really* be a bank robber? A billion-dollar bank robber? It sounded crazy, but every single clue matched. I decided to tell my mom and see what she thought.

"That's crazy," she said. "Look at this picture in today's paper."

She showed me the picture, a fuzzy still from footage taken by the bank's security cameras.

"It looks exactly like Casper with a mustache," I said.

"But Casper doesn't have a mustache," Mom said. "He's just a little boy."

"Actually, he's a slightly tall boy, and he does have a mustache—a fake one."

"Well, I think I know the difference between a fake mustache and a real one, and the bank robber's is real. Just look at it!"

I looked at it again. It did look completely real, but then again, so did the Heidelberg Handlebar Number Seven.

Thursday, Oct. 29, 5:30 P.M.

Dearest Lenny,

Man, did I get lucky today! When they closed school, I didn't have to go to math class, which was good because I hadn't done my math homework because I was "busy" last night.

I think I'm going to be "busy" again tonight, so, hopefully, they'll keep school closed tomorrow and I won't have to do that oral report on the Electoral College. Fingers crossed!

I remain as ever . . .

Your faithful friend,

Casper

The next morning, *Good Morning Hairsprinkle* reported that another bank had been robbed. A big government bank—the Hairsprinkle Federal Gold Reserve!

They were showing the same film clip over and over. It was from the bank's security cameras, and it showed a gang of school librarians breaking down the doors and knocking out the guards with ninja moves. Then a short mustachioed figure in a suit strode in and ordered them to blow the vault door off with dynamite and load the gold bricks onto book carts.

Actually, you couldn't tell they were school librarians from watching the video. But they were all arrested afterward and the police discovered that's who they were. One of them was Mrs. Minnick, our school librarian! Just like the accordion players, none of the librarians knew where the loot had gone or who the mustachioed man was.

The Hairsprinkle Federal Gold Reserve reported

that two billion dollars in gold had been taken. They said it would take fourteen big tractor-trailers to move all that gold.

Later in the morning, Move-U-Right Movers called the police to say that they were missing fourteen big tractor-trailers.

It was Friday, but school was called off for the whole day this time, and the National Guard was brought in to prevent another robbery.

My sisters and I had to stay inside all day, and by supper time they had just about driven me crazy.

So after supper—and another episode of *The Jodie O'Rodeo Showdeo*—I convinced my dad to let me go to Casper's house. He insisted on driving me over, even though it's only three houses away. Along the way, we passed several tractor-trailers driven by what appeared to be children's party clowns.

My dad dropped me off at Casper's and made me promise to phone him to pick me up instead of trying to walk home. "Remember, there's a mad genius criminal mastermind on the loose, and you never know where he might be," he said.

Actually, I was fairly sure that I DID know where the mad genius criminal mastermind was, but I didn't tell Dad that.

I rang Casper's doorbell.

"*Aw, you're just as welcome here as you can be, sugar,*" said Dolly Parton's voice.

A few moments later, Casper's mom answered the door. She was carrying what appeared to be a three-foot-long diseased carrot and she had a hatchet in her hand.

"Hey, Lenny. Wassup, dude? Casper's in his room. Supper will be ready at nine thirty if you want to stay . . ."

"Uh, no thanks, Tammy," I said. "I already ate."

I went up the stairs.

Casper was in his room, putting on a suit. But I noticed it looked slightly different from the one he had bought on our trip downtown.

"How do you like the pinstripes, Lenny?" Casper asked. "I decided the herringbone suit was a little too man-about-town and not quite enough hard-nosed businessman."

I couldn't think of anything to say, because just then I was looking at the rest of the room. The chair, his bed, and almost every bit of space was piled high with gold bricks and bundles of ten-thousand-dollar bills. There was no place to sit down.

"Red—the salesman at Chauncey's, remember?—he gave me another cravat. Honestly, I really don't need two. Would you like it?"

"No, I wouldn't," I said. "Listen, you've got to tell me what's going on! Did you rob the Federal Gold Reserve?"

"What Federal Gold Reserve?" he asked.

"The Hairsprinkle Federal Gold Reserve that got robbed!"

"Really?"

"Yeah, really, it's all over the news. The national news!"

"Huh, well, you know we don't have a TV, so I didn't see the news."

Just then the voice of Johnny Cash came floating through the house: *"Welcome to the house, man."*

Then Casper's mother hollered up the stairs. "Casper! There's a limo driver here for you."

"Shoot! I'll have to put the mustache on in the car," said Casper, placing the Heidelberg Handlebar Number Seven in his suit pocket along with the bag of spirit gum. "Sorry I don't have more time to talk. I've got to get to School Skate Night down at the roller rink."

"The roller rink closed last year," I said. "And you never went to School Skate Night anyway."

"Wish me luck!" he shouted, and he took off down the stairs.

"Did you do it or not?!?" I yelled after him.

He didn't answer.

When I got outside, his limo was racing away down the street. I flipped open my cell phone and called my dad to come pick me up. Then I called 911.

"Hairsprinkle Dispatch," said a voice, really fast but also bored.

"Yeah, I know who the bank robber is."

"Let me put you through to the FBI tip line," it said even faster and boreder.

This time I got a recording.

"The FBI is searching for a short man-about-town with a handlebar mustache. If you know any short men-about-town with handlebar mustaches, please rat them out at the tone. Beep."

"Yeah, I know who the bank robber is. His name is Casper Bengue, and he lives at 3414 Sprinkle Street, East Hairsprinkle. He's got all this money and gold in his bedroom . . ."

Suddenly, I started to feel really bad for turning in

Casper. I mean, he was my best friend before all this started. But then again, this was big. Not like the time he stole the thing that Mrs. Campbell uses to line the football field.

"Uh, come quick!" I finished, and hung up.

Yes, I had done the right thing, I decided . . . Maybe. But then I wondered if Casper would ever find out that I was the one who turned him in.

★ ★ ★

I worried about it all night. Whether I should have done it and what would happen when Casper was arrested and how mad he would be if he found out it had been me.

I never really got to sleep. I kept listening for police sirens racing toward Casper's house. Maybe even a police helicopter. At five A.M. I got dressed and went downstairs and turned on *Happy Weekend Hairsprinkle*. The anchorwoman was saying:

"Hairsprinkle breathes more easily after a quiet night. No arrest has been made, but no more banks have been robbed. We have FBI director Marcie Dropbag with us live from Hairsprinkle. You must be relieved, Director Dropbag."

"Relieved but frustrated, Angie. We spent the

evening following up on false tips from our tip line."

"False tips? What sort of sick person would phone in a false tip at a time like this?"

"I don't know, Angie, but it makes our job harder. Can you believe that one caller tried to turn in a seventh grader?"

"A seventh-grade teacher?"

"No, Angie, an actual seventh-grade student. The caller claimed this student had a bedroom full of 'money and gold.' We checked it out and, of course, found a typical messy bedroom full of smelly clothes and presidential action figures, but no gold or money."

"Director Dropbag, may I ask: Did the seventh grader even have a mustache?"

"Of course not, Angie. He did have a suit, but it was more of a hard-nosed businessman suit than a man-about-town suit. It was nothing but a waste of time and resources for the department."

"I'm sure all of our viewers are hoping you can trace the call and severely punish the person who made it."

"I wish we could, Angie, but there was some sort of glitch with the phone system, and that information wasn't recorded last night. But I've been told that it has been fixed, so if any more jokers are thinking of calling, I'd like them to know that I will personally track them down and destroy them with great pleasure! Ha-ha-ha-ha-ha-ha-ha!"

"Well, thank you very much, Director Dropbag."

"And thank you, Angie."

"Actually, my name isn't Angie, it's Nancy."

"Sorry, Nancy."

"That's OK, Director Dropbag."

"Call me Marcie."

"Marcie, are you ready to share your recipe for triple chocolate brownies?"

*G*adzooks! If the FBI had traced that call, I would have been arrested! Outrageous.

But what I couldn't understand is what DID happen to all that money Casper had in his room? I mean, it was billions of dollars. Where could it have all gone?

Then I heard Nancy the anchorwoman again.

"In other big news, the Heidelberg Novelty Company has been purchased in a cash transaction for a reported sum of two point four billion dollars. Sources say the new owner is billionaire hard-nosed businessman Fako Mustacho."

And they showed a picture of Casper wearing his mustache! Didn't they notice that the picture looked exactly like the one of the bank robber they were just talking about? And that name: Fako Mustacho? He was practically spelling it out for them!

But at least this explained where the money had gone.

The news went to split screen. Nancy was talking to one of those guys who looks like he knows everything.

"Welcome to the show, Barney. What can you tell us about billionaire hard-nosed businessman Fako Mustacho?"

"Never heard of him."

"Me neither, but I'm sure we'll be hearing a lot more from him in the coming days, Barney."

"Because he's so handsome?"

"No, Barney, because the Heidelberg Novelty Company is the world's largest manufacturer of voting machines, and the presidential election is just a few days away."

"Really? Wow."

I stopped listening. I was beginning to wonder about something. Even though the FBI hadn't figured out that I was the one who had called in the tip about Casper . . . maybe Casper had.

I mean, it must be obvious. I was in his room and saw the money. Then someone called the FBI and told them he had the money in his room. He must have known it was me.

But what would he do about it, I wondered. Would he be mad?

That's when our front door was knocked open by a battering ram and fast-food restaurant employees burst through, pointing at me and yelling, "There he is! The Evil One! Grab him!"

*L*uckily, I have spent many hours planning what I would do if someone broke into the house. True, I thought that it would be a burglar, not a horde of fast-food employees, but, still, it was a pretty good plan.

Step 1: Pick up sisters' Jodie O'Rodeo DreamDoll Mall Adventure set and hurl it toward door. This caught a fry cook in the nose and made a drive-thru cashier trip. (I could tell he was a drive-thru cashier because he still had on his headset.)

Step 2: Throw TV remote controls with ninja-like speed and accuracy. *Oof! Pow! Bam! Ouch!* All that practice paid off!

Step 3: Grab flat-screen TV off wall and bash it over their heads. (It turned out that the TV was bolted to the wall, so I went to the next step.)

Step 4: Head for kitchen. Run around counter, pulling open oven door for them to trip over.

Step 5: Grab any dirty dishes from sink and throw them like lethal Frisbees.

Step 6: While they duck dishes, reverse direction, use stool to jump onto counter, and run back toward living room, leaping easily over their heads, landing with a tuck and roll, and running out the still-open front door. (The tuck and roll didn't really work because I rolled right into Dad's recliner.)

Step 7: Jump over porch railing and land on bike.

Nobody can catch me when I'm on my bike.

O r at least nobody on another *bike* can catch me. I wasn't expecting someone on one of those little motorized scooters.

As I was pedaling toward the streetlight on the corner of Custer Street, I heard a whiny motor fire up. I looked back and saw the drive-thru cashier on a scooter. He was gaining fast.

I leaned hard to the right and hit my back-wheel brake to go into a skid, taking the corner fast and tight. Drive-thru took it wide and sloppy, but then he hit the accelerator and came flying after me.

I knew I couldn't beat the scooter on the open road.

I turned onto Morton Avenue, raced past one house, and turned up the alley to Broken Swing Park.

He was still behind me. I could hear him talking into his headset, calling for backup. I was pedaling as hard as I could, but he was gaining. That actually helped, because it was still pretty dark and the scooter's headlight showed me what I was looking for: the little gap in the fence around the McClains' backyard.

I shot through the gap and picked up speed fast. The McClains' backyard is a steep hill where everybody goes sledding in the winter. I was flying now, but the bumps made my teeth almost shake out of my head.

There's a creek at the bottom of the hill that goes right through the backyard, and I was aiming for the little wooden bridge that crosses it. But then I remembered Tony McClain's ramp.

Tony's a high school kid with a real BMX-type bike. He built a ramp to make jumps over the creek. He can do it pretty easy, and a couple of other bigger kids in the neighborhood have tried it, but I never have. I've thought about it and even tried to try it one time, but then I chickened out before I hit the ramp.

I didn't chicken out this time. It was just barely light enough for me to see the ramp, but I hit it dead center and at full speed. I had plenty of air over the creek. But I didn't have any idea how to land. The bike seat seemed to be moving away from me. If I landed like this, I'd bust my behind, so I pushed the bike away and got ready to land on my feet.

I tucked and rolled and almost broke my ankle.

I bolted up and started to reach for my bike when

I saw Drive-thru about to hit the ramp. He was going way too fast. If he hit the ramp, he'd kill himself.

"Look out, man!" I shouted, forgetting that if he killed himself, he wouldn't be able to kill me.

He swerved and braked, missed the ramp, and crashed into the creek. I knew this was my chance to get away, but it didn't seem right to leave him lying there. I peeked into the ditch.

The guy was staggering to his feet.

"Is this Burger King?" he asked.

"No! This is a ditch in the McClains' backyard, and you've crashed your scooter here in the wee hours of the morning while trying to kill me with your insane fast-food coworkers!"

"Do you want the value meal or just the Whopper?" he asked.

I was back on my bike in a second and out of there.

I wasn't checking my e-mail right then, obviously, but this message showed up in my in-box right around the time Drive-thru hit the creek. I didn't see it until much later, but I'm putting it here because it's important to the story.

Saturday, Oct. 31, 5:30 A.M.
Dear Sir,

I can't believe you tried to turn me in last night. That really hurt my feelings. I thought you were supposed to be my best friend. I'm too upset to write any more right now. My tears are dripping on the keyboard.

Boo hoo hoo!

Brokenhearted, but always . . .

Yours faithfully,

Casper Bengue

P.S. It's Halloween tonight. You want to meet at my house and go trick-or-treating?

I stopped pedaling like crazy when I was a few blocks away and realized nobody was following me anymore.

I had no idea where to go next.

My house was no longer safe. And it was Saturday morning, so I couldn't go to school. That wouldn't have been safe anyway. If Casper—aka the billion-dollar bank robber, aka Fako Mustacho—could somehow control school librarians, he could probably control teachers as well!

What exactly was he doing, I wondered. How did he get this power to make ordinary accordion players, librarians, truck drivers, party clowns, and fast-food employees turn into his henchmen and henchwomen?

Brainwashing? Hypnosis? Some kind of zombie-mind-power magic?

Whatever it was, that mustache must be the key.

It also meant I had no idea who might come after

me next. I saw a lady getting into her car to go to work. Was she going to come after me too? No, she didn't. But I had no way of knowing who was working for Casper. I could trust no one!

That gave me two options: I could hide in the woods, where I wouldn't have to worry about anybody, except maybe brainwashed forest rangers.

Or I could do what Casper had done and get a disguise. A disguise would allow me to keep an eye on things and try to figure out what Casper was up to. I mean, if I went off and hid in the woods, there would be no one to stop him from doing whatever it was he was doing.

It was hard to believe that Casper was really a bad guy. He had always been pretty nice to me. Maybe he had gone crazy. Either way, I had to get that disguise. And there was only one place I could think of to get it: Sven's Fair Price Store.

It was a long ride there on my bike.

By the time I got downtown it was 7:45, but Sven's hadn't opened yet. A sign said EXTENDED HALLOWEEN HOURS—8 A.M. TO MIDNIGHT. Today was Halloween, I realized. I would only have a little while to wait.

I went down a back alley and found a good place to hide my bike. There's a stream that runs through downtown, but it's mostly under stuff like parking lots and buildings. But there are a couple of places where it comes out into the open and you can see the tunnel-like place that it comes out of. I put my bike just a little way back into one of these, just far enough so that it would be out of sight. I didn't know when I'd be coming back for it. Depending on my disguise, I wasn't sure if I'd be able to ride the bike. If I got a disguise like a doctor, for instance, it would look suspicious if a doctor was riding around town on my bike, as awesome as it is.

I waited until eight o'clock and then went into Sven's.

*I*nside the store a weird guy was arguing with Sven.

"Where is the Heidelberg Handlebar Number Seven?" he yelled in what seemed like a European accent. Not exactly French but sort of French.

"I told you," Sven said. "I sold it a few days ago."

"To whom did you sell it?"

"I'm sorry, but all transactions are confidential."

"We'll see about that!" the man shouted, and he spun around and stomped out the door. I noticed two things about him. First, he already had a mustache, but it was thin and wispy, as if he had just started growing it. Second, he had the steel-gray, unblinking eyes of a professional assassin, full of cold, calm hate.

Then he stuck his head back in the door.

"By the way, is there a bicycle shop around here? I need a quick way to get around town without burning fossil fuels."

"The bike shop closed when Walmart came," said Sven.

"Oh. OK, thanks," the man said, and left.

*I*t wasn't until I was walking down the costume aisle that I thought about money.

I had fifty-three dollars saved up at home, which could have bought me a really, really cool costume of some sort—like a biker outfit with a helmet, goggles, and a jacket with SMELL'S ANGELS and a picture of a tattooed skunk with wings and a halo on the back.

But when I checked my pockets, all I had was that stiff ten-dollar bill Casper had given me. I had been planning on giving it to charity, since it was probably stolen, but now I needed it.

Even so, ten dollars wasn't going to get me much. Everything was at least $9.99, and with tax it would be more than ten.

But in the back of the store I found a pile of clearance costumes.

They were really, really lame. That's why no one had bought them in the first place. I mean, who would want a boxing hot dog costume? Or who would want to be a capybara? I like capybaras, but I wouldn't want to be one for Halloween.

Even if I had wanted to be a boxing hot dog or a large South American rodent, these wouldn't have made very good disguises.

Then I saw a cowboy hat, and I thought, Yeah, I could be a cowboy. But when I picked it up, I saw it had long pink hair coming out of it in two big ponytails or pigtails or whatever girls call them.

It came with a pink vest, a pink shirt, a pink skirt, and a pink guitar. The hat, the shirt, the vest, the skirt, and the guitar all had fancy sparkly writing on them that said JODIE O'RODEO.

I threw the costume down in disgust. It seemed really creepy to dress up like a girl that I have a crush on. Really creepy!

But it was only four dollars, and I couldn't find anything else.

I went up front to pay for it. Sven was running the register, and I was prepared for her to be nasty to me like the last time.

But she gave me a big smile when she saw what I was buying.

"Oh, you're buying the Jodie suit. That's so sweet. I'm Jodie's biggest fan."

"Me too," I said. "But this is for my sister."

Sven then talked for ten minutes about the time she saw Jodie in concert and almost got to give her a hug before some security guards grabbed her and wrestled her to the ground while Jodie sprinted for the tour bus.

"I know Jodie didn't mean it," said Sven.

"I'm sure she didn't," I lied.

"You seem like a nice boy," said Sven as she rung up the sale and counted out my change without even looking. "Didn't you buy one of those elastic sticky hands that's connected to a sort of sticky-stretchy rubber kind of thing the other day?"

"Yes, I did. It's really great!" I lied again.

"Well, looky what we just got in . . . the deluxe model!"

She held up an even bigger plastic egg, which presumably had an even bigger sticky hand inside. A sticker said SUPERLATIVE DELUXE GRABBER HAND! STRETCHES 20 FEET! The price was $8.95.

"That looks wonderful," I lied a third time, "but I don't think I have enough money."

"Money! Bah! What is money? Just pieces of paper. Never let money stand in the way of your dreams, kid. Never! Look at me. I lose thousands of dollars on this place every month. But I always say that the smiles on the faces are payment enough."

I smiled.

"So take the deluxe sticky hand! Go follow your dreams! In your darkest hour, it will be there for you. A beacon of hope and love!"

I took it. "Thanks. Hey . . . uh . . . do you mind if I use the changing room?"

"For the costume? I thought it was for your sister."

"Well, no, it's for me, actually."

"Follow your dreams! Never stop dreaming!" Sven sang out.

She handed me the key to the changing room, which was chained to a big piece of wood with glittery golden letters: LOSE THIS KEY AND I'LL RIP OFF YOUR FACE— SVEN.

When I got out of the changing room, Sven got one of her employees to take a picture of us together.

"You look just like her!" Sven shouted, and she gave me a big hug.

I could see why the real Jodie had run for her tour bus. But I was starting to like Sven. A little scary, but not likely to become an evil mastermind and send fast-food employees to kidnap me.

As I walked out the door, she waved. I think she was starting to cry.

★ ★ ★

I decided that it would be OK for Jodie O'Rodeo to ride a bicycle. People might expect her to ride a horse, but since she was a kid, I figured she might ride a bike sometimes.

So I went back through the alley and climbed down to where the stream goes under the streets.

My bike was gone!

But I could see a wet tire track leading farther into the tunnel.

Then I saw that someone had left a little note. "For

borrowing your bicycle I am very sorry! I will return it to you after I finish my mission of revenge and destiny!"

"Hey, bring back my bike!" I yelled into the tunnel, and it made a booming echo.

Then I started thinking about what would happen if the bike thief actually heard me and came back. I decided to get out of there.

Anyway, now that I had the disguise, I didn't really need the bike so much. It should be safe for me to walk down the street—or even ride the trolley.

I decided to go home and see what was going on there. My parents were probably worried when they noticed that the door had been busted open, the kitchen had been trashed, and I was missing.

I got on the trolley expecting everybody to go, "Oh, look! There's Jodie O'Rodeo!" Or worse, "Look! There's a boy dressed like Jodie O'Rodeo!" But that's not what happened.

Instead, everybody had this weird hypnotized look. A guy in a suit asked me, "Have you seen the Evil One?"

And a lady in a suit said, "If you do, you must capture him and take him to Fako Mustacho."

"Duh," I said. "I've known about that for hours. How did you find out?"

"I was lucky enough to see Fako Mustacho on the *Good Morning Hairsprinkle* show. He inspired me with his vision of a New World Order, and he shared his recipe for real Southern-style coleslaw—"

"Didn't you love the way he chopped that cabbage? He sure can handle a knife!" added a weird-looking guy who was eating potato chips.

"Yes! But my favorite part was when he warned us of the Evil One, a desperate bank-robbing criminal mastermind who is living in Hairsprinkle disguised as a boy named Lenny."

"It's terrifying to think the Evil One may be in Hairsprinkle right now!"

"It sure is," I said.

I couldn't believe it! Fako Mustacho—I mean, Casper—had somehow convinced everybody that *I* was the bank-robbing bad guy, not *him*, even though *he* was the one with the mustache!

I knew that my parents never missed *Good Morning Hairsprinkle*. But surely they wouldn't be fooled by Casper and his fake mustache and his lies about me . . . right?

When I got to my house, I saw that it was surrounded by cable installers. I could tell because they all had clipboards, tool belts, and big loops of coaxial cable.

"Halt, who goes there?" one of them said to me.

"It's me, Jodie O'Rodeo, preteen singing sensation and star of the recently canceled TV show *The Jodie O'Rodeo Showdeo.*"

"Was that on cable?"

"Yes."

"Basic cable or premium?"

"Premium."

"You may pass."

I went into my house. My parents and two cable guys were watching a *Good Morning Hairsprinkle* special bulletin and sobbing.

Nancy, the anchorwoman, was saying something like this:

"Heidelberg CEO and stylish hard-nosed businessman Fako Mustacho is on his way to address the governor and state lawmakers about the Lenny Junior crisis. Meanwhile, the crime wave has spread from Hairsprinkle to eight more cities, where teams of lumberjacks have robbed billions in cash and equipment from banks, jewelers, and dentist offices."

My mother wailed. "Oh, Lenny Senior, I can't believe our own son was really a master criminal disguised as our son."

"That makes no sense at all," said my father sharply. "He *is* our son. It just turns out that he's an evil bank-robbing creep."

"Oh, I thought he was just pretending."

"He *was* pretending," my father insisted. "Pretending to not be an evil bank-robbing creep!"

"Well, whichever, Mr. Smart Guy! Either way, he's broken my heart."

"Mine too, darling. I wish we had never named him Lenny Junior. He's a disgrace to the proud name Lenny Flem."

"Oh, Lenny Senior, why is TV star Jodie O'Rodeo in our living room?"

"I don't know, darling, I can only assume she was sent here by Fako Mustacho."

"Yes, that's right," I said. "Fako Mustacho sent me here to collect evidence."

"What sort of evidence?"

"Oh you know, Lenny Junior's cell phone, his wallet, some clean socks and underwear—that sort of thing."

"You go right ahead and take whatever Fako needs, little cowgirl! But first, can we get an autograph for our daughters . . . our beloved daughters, who are at a ballet lesson and are not robbing banks like their no-goodnik brother . . ."

I tried not to let all this hurt my feelings. They were brainwashed or hypnotized or something, after all.

I went up to my room and got all my stuff, like my cell phone and wallet. And I changed my socks. I like to have fresh socks whenever possible. I got my backpack, threw out my school stuff, and put in more socks and some makeup I stole from my sisters' room to make me look more like Jodie.

Then I went down to the kitchen and stuffed all the beef jerky and Vienna sausages we had into my backpack.

My parents were too busy watching news reports about me to notice.

*I*f you weren't paying attention in school, you may not know that Hairsprinkle is our state capital. The governor has her mansion and her office here, and the state lawmakers meet at a big Chinese buffet restaurant on the far side of town. They used to meet in our fancy gold-domed capitol building, but they kept trashing the bathrooms and got kicked out.

So now they meet in the back of Winston's Emerald Crown Buffet. Casper and I both went there on a field trip last year. We got to see the lieutenant governor eating these big cubes of Jell-O with chopsticks. He was really good at it. But we didn't actually see any laws get made or anything.

The TV had said Fako Mustacho was going to talk to all the government people at once. I figured he would probably do it there. So I hopped on the first crosstown trolley I saw.

I didn't know what I would do when I got to

Winston's, but at least I wouldn't be two steps behind Casper this time.

I was getting used to being Jodie O'Rodeo. The surprising thing was that nobody seemed surprised to see a hot-pink cowgirl on the trolley. Maybe they'd seen more cowgirls on the trolley than you'd think or maybe they were half hypnotized.

It's a long ride all the way across Hairsprinkle to Winston's. First, I checked my text messages on my cell phone. Most of my messages come from Casper and I didn't expect to have any from him. But I did have one!

Y U NOT @ CURLING PRACTIC 2DY?

I had forgotten all about practice. Casper and I are both on a local rec league curling team. I'm not so good, but Casper is the best slider in the state.

My first thought was, I'd better get down to the practice hut. But then I realized that Casper wasn't really at curling practice, he was on TV pretending to be Fako Mustacho. Wasn't he?

Or was it possible that he really was at curling practice and Fako Mustacho was someone else?

No, I reminded myself, it's impossible. Well, not impossible. But if Casper wasn't Fako, then where did the money come from? Or the limo? Or any of that stuff?

A much simpler solution was that Casper had sent this text message to fool me. He was good at fooling people, I realized. He fooled the police, my parents, the newscasters, and he was probably going to fool the governor next. I had to be careful and not get fooled too.

I'm the only one who seems to be immune to Casper's mustache power, I thought to myself, because I'm the only one who knows it's a fake.

For the rest of the ride, I checked out my new Superlative Deluxe Grabber Hand. It really was a lot better than the old one. I used it to pick up some trash from the floor of the trolley. Mostly breath-mint wrappers, but I got this one piece of paper about the size of a business card that said "Winston's Emerald Crown Buffet Platinum Club. Buy 364 buffet lunches and get ONE FREE."

It had only been stamped once. I guess whoever got it hadn't wanted to eat there every day for a year just to get a free lunch.

*W*hen the trolley got to the Winston's stop, I got off—but I couldn't see Winston's. There were so many people and police cars and T-shirt vendors and signs in the way.

It didn't take long to discover that every single one of these people was trying to get into Winston's and that they were all Fako fans.

They had buttons and T-shirts and umbrellas and temporary tattoos with Fako's picture on them.

How was it possible, I wondered, for all this stuff to have been made already? I stooped down to pet a dog wearing a THIS DOG'S FOR FAKO! doggy sweater. While the owner wasn't looking, I looked for the tag. It was sticking out near the dog's tummy.

"Does doggy want a belly rub?" I said loudly, and rolled the dog over. I read the tag. Just as I suspected!

"Made in Hairsprinkle, USA, by the Heidelberg Novelty Company. Do not dry-clean."

Actually, I didn't suspect the "do not dry-clean" part, but I had started to suspect that all this stuff had been cranked out by Heidelberg! It was just like when Heidi Timkin ran for class president and her father ordered six hundred hats that said TIMKIN on them in sparkly letters and everybody voted for her because her opponent, Sweaty Howell, didn't give out anything. The sad thing was: Sweaty would have been a great president.

Anyway, Casper-Fako was using the same idea to turn himself into a celebrity. Every T-shirt, every doggy sweater made him seem like more of a superstar. And every person who thought he was a superstar would want to have a T-shirt, and on and on.

But I couldn't see the point to it. He wasn't going to run for class president, was he?

So there I was in the big crowd, dressed like a cowgirl. How was I going to get inside?

Just then a really, really, really, really, *really* annoying person came along.

"OK, everyone, we need to clear a path here. Sir, could you clear a path here? Clear a path, please. We need to keep a path open. Clear a path, please. A path must be kept open. Ma'am? Clear a path, please. Have your dog clear the path, please."

And on and on and on. She never stopped talking. And no one cleared a path. So she'd really get in somebody's face and then they'd move over a foot, and she'd move on and they'd move back.

Finally, she got to me.

"Clear a path."

"I'm Jodie O'Rodeo."

"Please clear a path, Judy."

"No, it's Jodie! I'm famous! I'm a TV star!"

"You'll have to clear a path."

"What's the path for?"

"The path, which must be cleared, is for the governor, the state lawmakers, the media, and members of Winston's Emerald Crown Buffet Platinum Club."

I showed her my card.

"Can you clear the path for me, please?" I asked.

"With pleasure," she said, an evil gleam in her eye.

If she was annoying before, she was dangerous now. She wasn't just clearing a path for the sake of having a path. She now had a sacred duty to get me through the crowd to the restaurant. She dropped her phony politeness and started shoving people out of the way. She bulldozed a path for me all the way to the door.

It was really crowded inside. There didn't seem to be any chance of getting near the food. The line for egg drop soup looked about a mile long. I saw two old guys fighting over a chicken wing.

Just then a cook came out with a big tub of crab rangoon. That's my favorite. He was headed to the buffet with it. I knew I had to act fast or all that tasty deep-fried fake crabmeat would be gone in a second. But I couldn't get anywhere near the cook.

I figured I was about nineteen feet away. Luckily, the Superlative Deluxe Grabber Hand stretches twenty.

My first flick was perfect, but a famous TV news anchor walked in the way at the last second. The Grabber Hand bounced off her shellacked hairdo and came back empty.

There was time for only one more shot.

"Hey, Nancy from *Good Morning Hairsprinkle*! Watch out!" I shouted.

She leaned back just as the Grabber Hand shot past her, landed securely on a crab rangoon, and zipped back into my hands.

"Thanks, Nancy," I shouted. "My mom's a big fan of yours."

"And my niece is a big fan of yours, Jodie!" she called back.

We exchanged autographs and I split my crab rangoon with her.

Then I realized I was talking to a powerful TV journalist. If I could convince her that Casper was just a kid with a fake mustache, she could tell the whole world!

But at that moment a trumpet sounded.

"Make way! Make way for Fako Mustacho!" someone with a British accent shouted.

Fako himself was coming through the front door. He sure looked stylish and rich. And tall! Short for an adult but awfully tall for Casper. I craned my neck to get a look at his shoes. They were cowboy boots with six-inch soles. He could barely walk in them, but since he was surrounded by bodyguards on all sides, he didn't fall over.

I took a good look at the mustache. It really did look good, but maybe a tiny bit crooked. Maybe I'd be able to convince Nancy.

"Look, Nancy," I said. "That's a fake mustache!"

"Actually, Jodie, it's pronounced FAH-koh Mus-TOSH-oh. Excuse me, I think I see a chance to get some sweet pork on a stick. Want me to get you some?"

"No thanks," I said, too depressed to eat anything else.

H ear ye, hear ye!" shouted someone in a really deep, official-sounding voice. "The state legislature is now in session. The Honorable Fako Mustacho now presiding. Oopsie! I mean, the Honorable Governor Barbara Broom presiding . . . for now. Please take your seats in the back room. And, please, when visiting the buffet, take all you want, but eat all you take."

Luckily, I wasn't all that far from the hallway that led to the back room, so I was able to get a place to stand. It turned out to be right next to Lieutenant Governor Ken Wickle's table. He was shoveling Jell-O cubes into his mouth with chopsticks again.

"You've got to stop Fako Mustacho," I said. "He's a criminally insane kid with a fake mustache that robs banks."

"The fake mustache robs banks?"

"No, the insane kid robs the banks."

"But that's not what you said. You said, 'a fake

mustache that robs banks.' Even a cowgirl like you should know that grammar always counts."

"OK, fine. He's a criminally insane kid that robs banks."

"Oh, you mean Lenny Flem Junior."

"No, Lenny Flem Junior is innocent, Fako Mustacho is guilty."

"Guilty of robbing from himself?"

"What are you talking about?"

"Well, little lady, don't tell anybody yet, but the offices of the Heidelberg Novelty Company were robbed this morning. The thieves took seventeen billion dollars!"

"What? Why would the Heidelberg Novelty Company have seventeen billion dollars in their offices?"

"Well, it wasn't safe to keep it in the banks anymore, was it? They've got to keep it somewhere."

Hmmph! I wasn't buying it. It sounded like a clever trick on Fako's part. Now that he was a victim too, nobody would believe that he was the real bad guy.

The Heidelberg Novelty Company probably didn't even have seventeen billion dollars, unless it was money Fako had stolen.

"Greetings, my friends!"

I knew that voice well, even though Casper was trying to make his voice deeper than it really was.

"Greetings, Fako Mustacho," said the entire room, except me. Then the room became instantly silent. It didn't gradually die out as people finished sentences or cleared their throats. Just total silence.

I looked around. The people looked like zombies. The lieutenant governor had dropped his Jell-O cube and just sat there with the chopsticks dangling from his fingers.

I scooted over a little bit until I could see between the tall people.

Wow! Fako Mustacho ... so stylish ... so brilliant ... so hirsute . . . so trustworthy . . . I wish to serve him . . . so that all mankind may know the glory of his mustache. . . .

"WAIT!" A voice in my head screamed. "The mustache! It's fake! FAKE!"

That snapped me out of it. I turned away. The power of the mustache really was strong. I was afraid to look at Fako again.

So I just listened, and helped myself to the rest of the lieutenant governor's Jell-O. He didn't seem to mind.

Chapter 28

*F*irst, Fako Mustacho told the crowd that seventeen billion dollars had been stolen from his office that day.

"As you know, the Heidelberg Novelty Company is vital to the economy of Hairsprinkle, the United States of America, and the whole world. We're too big to fail. I was wondering if the state lawmakers would be willing to give us another seventeen billion dollars so we can stay in business."

A dude with a gavel jumped up. "All in favor say 'aye'!" he called.

Everyone in the room but me said "aye," even though half of them weren't state lawmakers.

"All opposed say 'nay,'" whispered the gavel dude.

I thought about saying "nay," but it would have made Fako suspicious of me, and all these brainwashed politicians would probably have torn me to pieces. So I just sat there.

The governor got up and wrote Fako a check on the spot.

"Thank you, governor. Thank you, my friends."

He put the check in his pocket.

"Now, let me first say a few words about Lenny Flem Junior."

The people around me started to shake and tremble. The lieutenant governor dropped his chopsticks.

"Evil One . . . Evil One . . . Evil One . . . ," the people whispered.

"Now, wait—wait just a second," said Fako. "I know that every piece of evidence points to Lenny Flem Junior being guilty of the string of crimes that has wiped out banks, companies, and governments. I know that every reasonable person who has watched the news believes that Lenny Flem Junior is guilty.

"But not *I*. I believe that in this great country of ours no one is truly guilty until they have been convicted in a court of law."

The crowd applauded and murmured about Fako's wisdom and goodness.

"So, until a judge passes judgment, let us not call Lenny Flem Junior a depraved monster heck-bent on destroying America, democracy, freedom, and the Heidelberg Novelty Company. Instead, let us catch him as fast as we can so we CAN convict him!"

"HOOOOWAAARRGGGHHHHH!" is about as close as I can get to putting into writing the sound the crowd made after that.

When people finally settled down, Fako continued. "The governor is a close friend of mine," he said. "I respect her and admire her. However, she hasn't been able to get the job done. She hasn't been able to catch Lenny Flem Junior."

"I'm really sorry," said the governor.

"I know you are," Fako said. "Would you mind resigning?"

"Not at all," she said, and she leaned forward and spoke into the microphone. "I hereby resign as governor of this great state. I have done my best to—"

"Hey! Let Fako talk!" somebody hollered.

"Quit hogging the mic, Babs!" shouted the lieutenant governor.

So Fako started up again, and in a few minutes he had been appointed governor by a unanimous vote of the state lawmakers.

Everybody but me cheered, and then Fako's bodyguards escorted him out of the building.

"Uh, excuse me," I said to the lieutenant governor, "but if the governor resigns, I thought that it was your job to take her place."

"Where's my Jell-O?" he snarled.

I walked back to the trolley stop in a daze.

Casper had me beat every step of the way. Now it wasn't just my word against his; it would be my word against the governor's!

What could I do? How could I stop him?

I might as well give up and go home. I'd have to wear the Jodie O'Rodeo disguise for a while, but Casper would probably forget all about me soon. I was too insignificant and pathetic and tiny to cause him any trouble.

I got on the trolley and found a seat. I was so burdened by the weight of being the lone voice against an evil madman that I didn't notice that someone was glaring at me.

"Who the ding-dang-day are you?" she said.

"I'm Jodie O' Rodeo," I said. "Preteen cowgirl queen."

"The hot heck you are! *I'm* Jodie O'Rodeo," she snarled. "And now I'm a TEEN cowgirl queen, thank you not so very much!"

It really was her. She was wearing an outfit just like mine, except with real cowboy boots.

And she was beautiful. She had been cute when her show was filmed a couple years ago. But now . . .

"Wow," I said. "You're beautiful."

"Well," she said, without so much snarl. "Thanks, but I'm afraid you're not. Your makeup looks terrible, and your hair looks like one of those awful wigs from the Heidelberg Novelty Company."

"It is."

"Well, that's OK," she said, sitting down next to me. "I'm flattered that you're going to be me for Halloween tonight. The truth is that most kids have forgotten about me now that my show is in reruns. They all want to be Roxy Diamond this year."

"Actually, I forgot it was Halloween tonight," I said. I knew it was risky to tell her my big secret, but at the same time I knew it wasn't. I could just tell that I could trust her. "I hope you don't mind, but . . . I've been in disguise as you all day because a mad lunatic has been sending his brainwashed henchmen to try and catch me."

"Oh, you must mean Fako Mustacho," she said.

"Yes! But how did you know?" I whispered, looking around to see if anyone was listening. The rest of the passengers, who all seemed to be bodybuilders, were just staring blankly out the windows.

"It's simple," she said. "Nobody ever heard of Fako Mustacho until a few days ago. Now he's rich, famous, and all over the TV. They even preempted one of my reruns with a special report about him. But he's nothing but a giant liar. He's just a kid with a fake mustache. I've been trying to tell my parents that ever since he showed up on TV. And not only is he a kid with a fake mustache, he's the same kid with a fake mustache who robbed all those banks."

"Wow," I said. "It's great to finally meet someone else who isn't fooled by his mustache."

"It really is," agreed Jodie. "Unfortunately, we've been fooled by something else. Look!"

I looked out the window.

I saw old brick warehouse-type buildings that I had never seen before. We weren't rolling down Hair Avenue through the heart of downtown Hairsprinkle.

"They switched the track on us!" said Jodie.

"This must be one of the abandoned freight lines that used to run to the factories down by the docks," I said. "We've got to get off."

The other passengers, who really *were* bodybuilders, stood up and growled at us.

"Sit down, Evil One!" said a guy with tattoos and a long ponytail. "We know that one of you is the Evil One and the other is a famous preteen cowgirl queen, but we don't know which one is which."

"Don't get us wrong," chanted the rest of the body-builders. "You are both pretty as a picture, but one of you is pure evil. So sit down!"

We sat down and they sat down.

There was some clacking and lurching and the trolley turned off onto a side track. The track led right up to a great big factory. The biggest one I'd ever seen.

There were giant letters on the side of the factory that read HEIDE BE G NOVELT C MPA Y.

"Jodie, I've got to get out of here," I whispered. "If Fako catches me, there'll be nobody to stop him."

"What about me? Maybe I can stop him."

"You shouldn't get involved. They'll let you go when they discover you're the real Jodie."

The driver blew the trolley whistle, and big, thirty-foot-high doors in the side of the factory slid open. The trolley started to roll inside. That gave me an idea. A crazy idea. A million-to-one idea. But at least it was an idea.

"I've got a crazy, million-to-one idea," I told Jodie. "Stay here and brace yourself against the seats. I'm going to force my way up there, throw myself against the control lever, speed up the trolley, and crash through whatever is waiting for us up ahead. In the carnage and confusion, I'll slip out the door. Oh yeah—when I push the control lever, I'm also going to open the door handle. And I guess I'd better—"

"That's the dumbest thing I've ever heard," said Jodie. "Why not just let me pretend to be you and you keep pretending to be me? That way they'll let you go. And if I get in any real trouble, I can easily prove that I'm really me, not you pretending to be me."

This was so confusing I could barely follow it. I was just starting to understand when the trolley passed through the big doors and stopped inside a cavernous room stacked with thousands of boxes.

Jodie stood up and announced, "I'm the Evil One. Please escort me to the front of the trolley so I can meet my fate like a man."

"Thank you," I whispered. "You're amazing. I hope I get to meet you again someday."

"Me too," she said. "I'd give you a good-bye hug if it wouldn't be so weird to hug somebody who looks like me. Or actually, I mean someone that I'm pretending to look like."

I didn't understand that either, but that may have been because I went into shock when she said the word "hug." I may have had a vague crush on TV Jodie, but it had turned into something a lot bigger for the real-life Jodie.

"Wait a second," said one of the bodybuilders. "How do we know this one isn't Jodie O'Rodeo and the other one isn't the Evil One?"

A collective "Duhhh, I dunno," went up from the

bodybuilders. If all this was confusing to me, it was clearly even more confusing to the bodybuilders, who, on top of spending too much time in sweaty places, were also brainwashed.

Jodie was way ahead of them.

"For one thing," she said, "my hair is just a wig."

She took off her cowgirl hat, and, lo and behold, her long braids were just as fake as mine. Her real hair was short and purple. Pretty cute, I thought.

"And for another thing," she said, "the real Jodie can yodel. Can't you?"

"Sure," I said. And I yodeled just like Jodie does on TV.

"Yo-day-low-day-yoda-lady-who, yo-day-low-day-yoda-lady-who. Yoda-lady-who. Yo-do-diddley-do, do-day-lady-day-do, diddle-di-dodo, diddley dodo, day. Little old lady who. Little old lady who. Little old lady, little old lady, little old lady who. Old lady, old lady, old lady, moo, old lady, too, old lady foo. Yoda hoda, biddli mocha, armadillo, too. Fiddle-dee-do-de-day di diddle dee way, no way, way. May, fay, hay, day—DAY! Diddle-dee-do-da-DAY! Diddledeeeeeeeeeeeeeeeeeeeeeeeeeeeeeeeeeeee eeeeeeeeeeeeeeeeeeeeeeeeeeeeeeeeeeeeeeeeeeeeeeeeeee eeeeeeeeeeeeeeeeeeeeeeeeeeeeeeeeeeeeeeeeeeeeeeeeeee eeeeeeeeeeeeeeeeeeeeeeeeeeeeeeeeeeeeeeeeeeeeeeeeeee

eeeeeeeeeeeeeeeeeeeeeeeeeeeeeeeeeeeeeeeeeeeeeeeeeeeeee
eeeeeeeeeeeeeeeeeeeeeeeeeeeeeeeeeeeeeeeeeeeeeeeeeeeeee
eeeeeeeeeeeeeeeeeeeeeeeeeeeeeeeeeeeeeeeeeeeeeeeeeeeeee
eeeeeeeeeeeeeeeeeeeeeeeeeeeeeeeeeeeeeeeeee-DO-DAY!
Hey!"

The bodybuilders applauded wildly.

*T*he bodybuilders asked me very nicely to wait on the trolley, and then they took Jodie away. The trolley driver just sat there. I guess the problem with using brainwashed henchmen is that they just sit around like idiots after they've done their job. Either that or the trolley driver really was an idiot.

I cleared my throat. I yodeled a bit more. I stood up. I moved one seat back. The driver never budged.

So I just got up and went out the back door.

Like I said, the loading room was stacked to the rafters with cardboard boxes. In between piles of boxes there were little trails and paths. In some places the path was more like a tunnel through the boxes.

I ran for one of the tunnels and crawled out of sight. In a few minutes those bodybuilders were going to be back down here looking for me.

You may have noticed that I didn't run away like Jodie told me to. There were two very good reasons.

First, I wanted to be sure that Jodie got out safely. I wasn't so sure that Casper-Fako was going to just let her go.

Second, if I left, I'd be no better off than I was before. Fako would be taking over the world and I would be on the run.

What I needed to do was use this chance to spy a little. Find out what his next plan was and figure out a way to stop it.

But if I was going to stay there, I couldn't keep wearing the Jodie O'Rodeo costume. But if I took it off, I'd be recognized as the real Evil One.

What I needed was a new disguise, I decided. Where could I get one?

That's when I noticed that every box around me was labeled HEIDELBERG NOVELTY COMPANY. I found a box that was sort of loose and carefully pulled it out of the stack. It was kind of like playing Jenga.

I opened it up: plastic scrambled eggs.

The next box: blue monster fingers.

Then green monster fingers in the one after that.

I found stink bombs, T-shirts that said MY PARENTS WENT TO HAIRSPRINKLE AND ALL I GOT WAS THIS LOUSY T-SHIRT, voting machines, trick gum, a pooh-pooh noise whistle and, at last, a deluxe teen werewolf costume.

It was pretty nice. It had fake eyebrows, fake ears, fake sideburns, a fake goatee, fake fur-covered mittens, and fake teeth. It even had a fake cardigan sweater, because teen werewolves are supposed to wear sweaters for some reason.

It didn't seem like a perfect disguise, but it was Halloween, after all, so if I got caught I could always pretend to be a trick-or-treater.

And I was glad to get out of the Jodie O'Rodeo outfit.

I looked at my watch. It was already 3:30. I had been a girl for more than seven hours!

I heard a ruckus out in the main part of the room.

I crept forward just enough to see what was going on.

The bodybuilders were back, along with three mimes.

"Where's the Evil One?" one of the mimes shouted at the trolley driver.

"Uh, the bodybuilders took him."

"No, you fool," shouted another mime. "That wasn't the real Evil One. The *real* Evil One was sitting here on your trolley and you let him get away."

"Sorry."

"You'd better be," snarled the third mime.

The bodybuilders immediately started searching. I realized that sooner or later they would find me and I would look pretty suspicious hiding in the middle of all these boxes.

I had to do something. I realized that all day long I

had been running and hiding, while Casper had been playing it cool and coming out ahead every time.

So I decided to try Casper's way.

I stood up and walked out from the rows of the boxes. I went right up to the three mimes. "Have you caught the Evil One yet?" I asked.

"No, these idiots let him get away. They brought us a washed-up former celebrity cowgirl instead."

"I guess you had to let her go, huh?" I asked.

"We will, but first we're going to plant a camera in her cowgirl hat. If she meets up with the Evil One again, we'll catch him for sure."

"Wow," I said. "You guys are really smart."

I headed for the doors I had seen them take Jodie through earlier. I came out into a long, empty hallway. There was an elevator partway down the hall. I pushed the button. While I was waiting, I decided to peek through the big double doors across the way.

Inside was a huge factory floor with lots of machines and wires and conveyor belts. There was this big system of chutes that seemed to be carrying liquid snot. A machine nearest me had doors that slammed closed every few seconds. Then there'd be a whooshing sound. Then the doors would open again, and a whoopee cushion would fall out onto a conveyor belt.

It was awesome. I could have looked at it all day, but the elevator doors opened behind me, and I ran back across the hall and got into the elevator.

I pushed the close-door button, then took a moment to look at my options. There were buttons for floors one through four and a basement. I figured the important offices would be on the top floor, so I pressed four.

When the doors opened again, I stepped out into a brightly lit hallway with people crisscrossing to and from rooms on either side. A few glanced at me, but I guess it takes more than a werewolf costume to attract attention in a novelty factory.

A sign on the door of the first room I came to said WHOOPEE CUSHION TESTING DEPARTMENT, and sure enough, lots of nasty noises were coming out. The next room said VOTING MACHINE RIGGING DEPARTMENT. I peeked through the window and saw a whole room full of geeks drinking Red Bull and messing with computers.

The next door said FAKO MUSTACHO, CEO. PRIVATE. KEEP OUT. CLEARANCE LEVEL ZED ALPHA ONLY. I tried to act cool and walk through the door like I belonged there. But the door was locked. And I felt kind of dumb.

The next room said RESEARCH AND DEVELOPMENT. This door was open and the room looked empty—empty of people, at least. It was crammed full of mad scientist–type stuff. I decided to check it out.

I walked in and suddenly—ZAMMO!—something hit me right between the eyes. I dove for cover and felt my face with my hand to see if I was bleeding. No blood, just a sticky residue and one furry eyebrow. The other teen werewolf eyebrow was gone.

"Ah, looks like I caught me a wolfman," cackled a voice that sounded like a toasted gravel sandwich.

I looked up and saw an ancient, three-foot-tall man walking toward me.

"Sorry to scare you, wolfboy," he said, "I was just testing out the new Ultra-Sticky-Stretchy Grabber Hand. I got your eyebrow from twenty-seven feet away whilst hiding behind the jukebox. Would you like it back?"

"Yes, sir," I said, and tried to stick it back in place.

"How do you do," the man said, offering his hand, "I'm Hank Heidelberg."

"Wow, you mean Heidelberg . . . like the Heidelberg Novelty Company? Did you start this company?"

"Yes, I did. Seventy-two years ago, my brother, Tito, and I were just kids like you peddling rusty kazoos on the streets of Nairobi. Then I invented the first sticky-stretchy hand. And the rest is history."

"Look," I said. "I've got one of your sticky-stretchy hands myself."

"Ah! You're a guy who knows a quality sticky-stretchy hand when you see one. Yes, that one was good, but I've never stopped working to perfect my invention. Please check out my latest version."

He made a small movement with his real hand, and I

saw a neon purple blur as the sticky hand shot across the room and grabbed a pink piece of paper. Then the sticky hand snapped back, bringing the pink paper with it.

"And look at this," he said, peeling the pink paper loose from the hand and showing it to me. "Just look at this . . ."

Then he started sobbing.

I looked at the paper. It said:

DEAR DR. HINK HIDDLEBURG,

FAKO MUSTACHO, THE NEW OWNER, PRESIDENT, AND CEO OF THE HEIDELBERG NOVELTY COMPANY, HAS ASKED ME TO INFORM YOU THAT YOUR SERVICES ARE NO LONGER REQUIRED. YOUR LAST DAY OF WORK WILL BE OCT. 31. PLEASE LEAVE THE BUILDING BY 5 P.M. OR OUR VERY RUDE SECURITY PERSONNEL WILL ESCORT YOU OUT.

YOURS TRULY,

BRAINWASHED HUMAN RESOURCES ASSISTANT #5

"My stars," I said, "Casper . . . I mean, Fako . . . has really changed. For years he had nothing but the highest respect for novelty product inventors. And now he's treating you like fake dog poo."

"I've been so busy in my lab, I hadn't even heard about this new owner. Do you know him?"

If Dr. Heidelberg hadn't seen Fako on the news, perhaps I would be able to tell him the truth.

"Fako Mustacho is just a kid wearing one of your fake mustaches. He's used it to rob banks, brainwash people, and get himself made governor!"

"Hmmm. A fake mustache, you say? Was it the Heidelberg Handlebar Number Seven, by any chance?" asked the old man.

"YES! How did you know?"

"I always feared that the Heidelberg Handlebar Number Seven was too good. My brother was at the height of his talents when he made it. It is one of a kind, you know. There is only one Number Seven. Tito died after making it—his life's work was complete. It was his masterpiece. But it was woven from the hairs of a very bad man who gave up his mustache unwillingly."

"Unwillingly?"

"Yes, he was a professional assassin, famous in the European criminal underworld for his perfect record of three hundred kills and for his perfect mustache. Then he was betrayed by a beautiful woman and arrested. When he arrived at prison, they shaved his mustache.

"I'm a scientific man, but still I felt that such a mustache would be better off in the trash. But my brother insisted on using it. 'It is too beautiful, too perfect,' he argued. 'Yes,' I would say, 'it is too perfect and it will be too powerful, especially if it falls into the wrong hands.'"

"It *has* fallen into the wrong hands," I said. "Fako Mustacho seems unbeatable. My best hope was to sneak in here and try to find out his secret plans. But his office was locked."

"You mean the CEO's office just down the hall? That used to be my office. I think I still have the key."

He pulled a key ring out of his pocket. Have you ever seen someone who has a lucky rabbit's foot on their key ring? Well, Dr. Heidelberg had some kind of white furry foot on his key ring, but it was way too big to be from a rabbit. I was afraid to ask what it was. A polar bear maybe? Or a yeti? Really gross.

He tried to get the key off but couldn't.

"Just take the whole ring," he said. "I won't be needing them anymore. Here, this one is for the CEO's office. I'd come with you, but I only have five more minutes before five P.M., when the security guards are coming for me."

"Thanks, Dr. Heidelberg. I hate to ask, but do you have any kind of secret weapon around here that might help me defeat Fako?"

"Sure. Here's a Nasal Gun. It enables you to shoot fake

boogers out of your nose. And here's some trick gum that shocks people's fingers when they touch it. And here's an edible eraser shaped like a dead chicken. And here's a LaughBomb. Pull the pin, throw it, and when it lands, it plays a recording of someone laughing really loud.

"And, since you are a wolfman who appreciates quality sticky-stretchy hands—I want you to have the Ultra-Sticky-Stretchy Grabber Hand too. I have not yet explored its full capabilities. Use it only for good."

I wasn't sure how any of that stuff was going to help me stop a crazy bank-robbing governor from brainwashing the whole human race, but I could tell it would make the old man feel better if I pretended it was great.

"I guess you'd better get out of the building, huh, Dr. Heidelberg. It's almost five!"

"Oh, no, you've misunderstood me. I won't be leaving the building."

"But the security guards! They're tough guys! Bodybuilders and mimes!"

"Doesn't matter," he said. "They'll never take me alive." And he strapped a Nasal Gun to his face and hid behind the jukebox.

"Good luck, Doctor!" I said, saluting the great man.

"And good luck to you, young wolfboy," he said, returning the salute.

I went back into the hall. The bodybuilders were coming, led by two mimes.

For a second, I thought I was done for. Then they stomped right past me and into Dr. Heidelberg's office.

I heard a soft *fizz, fizz* . . . then, "AGGGHHH!" screamed one of the mimes. "He shot a booger in my eye!"

A giant ruckus began with shouts, crashes, and the occasional *fizz, fizz* sound.

People came running from the other rooms to see the action.

I wanted to help Dr. Heidelberg, but I realized that the fight was the perfect distraction. No one noticed as I unlocked the CEO's door and slipped into the office.

It wasn't very nice, for a CEO's office. No windows, no carpet, just a drafting table, a desk, and an adjustable chair.

I looked at a few of the papers on the desk.

"Inauguration Planning" was written on one folder.

That's odd, I thought. I just saw his swearing in as governor this morning. It wasn't much of an inauguration and couldn't have taken much planning.

I opened the folder and then I understood.

National Mall . . . the Capitol . . . Pennsylvania Avenue.

It wasn't about his swearing in as governor, it was about his swearing in as president. President of the United States of America! Now I understood why he had bought the Heidelberg Novelty Company. It wasn't just for the mustaches—it was for the voting machines.

Election Day was on November 3, just three days away! And somehow Fako Mustacho was going to get himself elected president.

Behind me, the door opened. I tried to duck behind the desk, but it was way too late.

"Oh, hey! Lenny Junior! How's it going?"

I peeked over the desk. It was Casper! Or was it Fako Mustacho?

"Hey, dude," he said, still standing in the doorway. "I wish I could chat, but do you know who's downstairs? Jodie O'Rodeo! I always had a crush on her. And she's here! I gotta get down there before her taxi comes. I'll see if I can get you an autograph!"

It took me about 2.8 seconds to shake off the effects of seeing his mustache in person and spring into action.

"Make yourself at home up here until I get back," he was saying when I finally did leap over the desk, sorta ninja style, and lunged for the door. But I was 2.8 seconds too late. He closed the door while I was still leaping, and while I was lunging I heard the sound of his key turning in the lock. I grabbed the doorknob anyway, yanking and turning and yelling and banging on the door.

"See you later, Lenny Junior," he called cheerfully.

And I was trapped . . . a prisoner of my ex–best friend Casper Bengue, aka Fako Mustacho.

*W*ait! I still had the keys! But, no, there was no keyhole on this side of the door.

There were no windows and no other doors.

There was a telephone. I picked it up. Yes!

I called my house. My mom answered.

"Mom! I've been captured by Fako Mustacho! He's holding me prisoner at the Heidelberg Novelty Company!"

"Oh, good! I really think it's the best thing for you. Your father and I have been so upset about your bank-robbing spree. I know you kids like to rebel, but Fako Mustacho is our governor now and deserves your respect. Maybe if you stop acting like the Evil One, he'll give you some little jobs to do. That would look great on your college applications, wouldn't it? Sort of like an internship. I hear that—"

ZZAP!

I didn't hang up on her . . . Really. The phone

suddenly went dead. Casper must have remembered that it was in here and had someone cut the line. Not that it mattered. I never would have been able to convince her. And I had a feeling my dad would have said the same things.

I realized I still had my cell phone in my pocket. But who could I call? My parents wouldn't help me. The police wouldn't help me. Fako Mustacho seemed to have taken over the whole town. No, the whole state! And soon it would be the whole country.

Everybody seemed to be against me.

Well, except for one person. Jodie.

If I only knew her phone number! Or her e-mail address!

I was sure Jodie O'Rodeo had her own website, so I thought maybe I could guess what her e-mail address would be.

I sat down and started entering every e-mail address I could think of into a blank message.

Jodie@jodieorodeo.com
Jodieorodeo@jodieorodeo.com
Jorodeo@jodieorodeo.com
Fanmail@jodieorodeo.com

And so on . . .

Then I wrote and sent my message.

My cell phone said it was 5:13 P.M. What a day! I'd been running around like crazy for twelve hours and all I'd had to eat all day was part of a crab rangoon and some of the lieutenant governor's Jell-O.

Suddenly, I remembered that I had stashed all those Vienna sausages and beef jerky in my backpack. I decided to ration them out, since I didn't know how long I would be locked in.

After I ate a bit, I dumped a bunch of papers on the floor to make a bed and lay down to try to get some sleep.

*J*ust as I was about to get to sleep, my cell phone buzzed. NEW TXT MSG.

BEST. DAY. EVER. MET JODIE. THNK SHE
LIKES ME. I LIKE HER. IF U C HER AGAIN WILL
U ASK HER IF SHE LIKES ME? SORRY CANT
TRICKRTREAT 2 NITE. BIT BUSY. L8R, CASPER

After that, I couldn't get to sleep for a long time. But it didn't matter. I was a prisoner in a fake-mustache factory. I could sleep late the next day. And maybe the next and maybe the next and maybe . . .

PART II

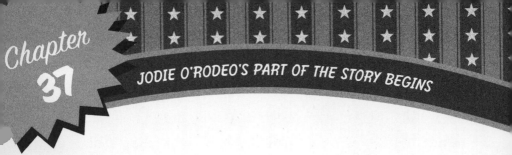

*H*ey, everybody, it's me, Jodie O'Rodeo.

This whole thing is pretty crazy, huh? I mean, if this was the plot to an episode of *The Jodie O'Rodeo Showdeo,* you'd be like, "Jodie's totally lost it."

Well, hold on, because it's about to get all jacked up like you wouldn't believe!

But you're just going to have to wait a minute.

I'd better start back where Lenny left off.

While he was being held prisoner, that creepy ex-friend of his, the so-called Governor Fako Mustacho, escorted me out of the building. He tried to act like he was a gentleman, not a dipwad with a fake mustache. I think he was trying to hit on me. No ding-dang way, you creep!

I was so happy to get away from that guy and into a taxi and back home.

I tried to tell my parents about what happened, but I think they were brainwashed from watching too much *Good Morning Hairsprinkle.* They just loved Fako Mustacho.

So that was pretty much it. What could I do? I didn't know how to reach Lenny. In fact, back then I didn't even know his name was Lenny Flem Jr.

I went out to feed my horse, Soymilk. Yes, Soymilk is really my horse, not just a TV character.

When we moved back to Hairsprinkle from Hollywood, I said no way was I going to leave Soymilk behind. Luckily, there was enough TV money left for my parents to buy this house, which has a small stable and enough room for Soymilk to run around a bit.

My parents may not have clue one about what's going on, but I can always talk to Soymilk.

I told her about Fako and the Heidelberg factory, but mostly I told her about Lenny Jr. The only problem was, like I said, I didn't even know his name back then.

"I met this really great guy," I told her. "It was like we became friends instantly. And he wasn't like all the kids at school who want to be my friend just because I was on TV. He seemed like a real friend.

"Of course, it's kind of hard to tell what someone is like when they are dressed up like you, but I thought he seemed really cute and smart and kind . . . and that yodel of his sounded so beautiful and yet so lonely . . ."

Soymilk understood. I can always tell if she thinks I'm right or if she thinks I'm crazy.

"I don't know if I'll ever see him again, though. But I am glad I helped him escape. I wonder where he went and what he's doing."

Soymilk didn't know either.

I went back in the house for supper. My mom asked me if I would take my brothers trick-or-treating.

"Whoa back!" I said. "What did I do to deserve this chore?"

"Just because you're a big star doesn't mean you're not still a big sister! Besides, you'll probably have fun."

That seemed unlikely, but I didn't have anything better to do, so I went. And as predicted, it stunk. The twins are hyperactive little boogers, especially when they've eaten a pound of candy.

The next day, Sunday, was more of the usual—hanging around the house, taking care of Soymilk, and avoiding the twins.

When I was in Hollywood, there was always something going on, like learning lines for the show, practicing stunts with Soymilk, or getting my picture taken for Jodie O'Rodeo licensed products. But now . . . Nothing!

After supper, I got so bored that I decided to check my e-mail. Lots of times I put it off, because it's kind of dangerous to my mental health. Sometimes it cheers me up; sometimes it makes me feel terrible.

A few years ago I got thousands of messages every day, and somebody on the TV show staff would pick out twenty or so and print them out for me and I would skim over them. Maybe.

But now that the show is in reruns I get just a few. And half of those usually say "You suck!" What makes people decide to send someone an e-mail like that? What makes them decide to make someone else feel bad? I got so many "You suck"s on my Facebook page, I decided to just delete it. And you wouldn't even believe the nasty stuff I got on Twitter.

I came close to deleting my e-mail address too, but the e-mails that don't say "You suck" usually make me feel good. They're from kids who still watch reruns or DVDs of the show and really like it. And they want to know stuff like, can I really rope a cow and ride a horse. And I always write back and tell them "Yes, I can" and suggest that they take horseback riding lessons or join Girl Scouts or 4-H and learn to do stuff too.

The funny thing is that nobody ever asks "Was that really you singing?" Everybody just assumes I can sing but can't do anything wild and exciting. But it's really the other way around. The singing was fake and the stunts were all real.

The truth is, the ding-dang TV show people wouldn't let me do half the cool cowgirl stuff on the show that I really can do, like barrel racing and hog-tying an ornery calf. Most of the plots were set in shopping malls and all I did was ride in, buy clothes, and then pretend to sing some song that was more electronic than cowgirl.

The other thing about me that was fake were the stories about me dating all these Hollywood stars and stuff. I met a lot of those guys at parties, but I didn't really like them or the parties. The parties weren't even real parties where people have fun. Instead, some publicist made me go and another publicist made some famous dude go. And we had to stand there and be all "I liked that movie you did with the talking dog."

And while we were standing there pretending to be happy, someone would take a picture, and then that picture showed up in a magazine saying I had another new boyfriend! But really I didn't have any boyfriends. Or any real friends either, but I didn't find that out until after the show was canceled.

So, anyway, it's nice to hear from a couple of kids who still like the show. It makes it feel like all that crazy stuff was worth it. Because most of the time, other than all the money we got, it doesn't.

The e-mails I got were:

Three "You suck"s. They didn't all say exactly that, but that was the main idea.

And there was a weird message from somebody's cell phone. The subject line said "Help!"

It looked like spam, but I decided to check it out.

TO: jodieomail@jodieorodeo.com
SUBJECT: help! im being hld prsoner n fake mustch factry!

i dnt knw wht u cn do but I dnt knw who else 2 ask. Parnts + police wont hlp. brainwshed by fako.

mybe u cn brng me sum food 2mrrw? flat enuff to fit under door. Not beef jrke pleez. Im n ceo offic. top floor.

nice 2 meet u 2day!!!

btw fako rggng elction trying 2 tke ovr whle wrld!

your pal lenny

Holy hamburgers! He didn't get away after all! That was my first thought. Then: His name is Lenny. And he liked meeting me! And then: And Fako wants to take over the world.

I hit reply:

Don't worry, Lenny, I'll do better than bring you some flat food. I'm going to get you out of there. Right now!

And it was REALLY nice meeting you too.

See you soon.

Your pal,

Jodie

XOXOXO

I wasn't 100 percent sure if I should add the XOXOXO part, but I couldn't help it.

I told my mom I had to go out. There was a big whoop-de-do about it, and my mother said her usual line: "Just because you're a big star doesn't mean you don't have to get up for school tomorrow morning."

"It's only eight o'clock," I said. "I'll be back by bedtime."

That turned out to be a total lie, but I didn't know it then.

I raced back to my room to get ready. I put on my riding clothes and grabbed some other things I thought I might need: lasso, fence-mending tool, throwing knives, and the sequined holsters with the pink pistols I used in one of the episodes. They only shoot water, but they are totally real-looking movie props. They might fool those idiots at the factory, I thought.

I have to admit that I spent a few extra seconds deciding which leather jacket to wear. I wanted to look my best when I saw Lenny again. I picked the long black one with the fringe and the beaded black cat on the back. Seemed like the right thing to wear when you're about to break bad.

Wearing a backpack messed up the effect a little bit, but I needed a way to carry all my stuff. Plus, I brought along a bunch of Pop-Tarts for Lenny.

I put on my hat and headed to the stable.

"Hey, sweetie," I said, "are you ready for a wild ride?"

Soymilk snorted. She's a smart horse. She could tell I was serious.

"No time for the saddle tonight," I told her. "We'll do it bareback, just like the old days."

She snorted again.

"Hey-YO-yo-te-do, let's go!"

Soymilk's horseshoes rang and sparked on the pavement as we hurtled out of my subdivision, scattering some kids who were busting pumpkins in the street.

"Look out, ya little woolbusters!" I yelled. "I got a license to fly."

It's several miles from my house to the Heidelberg factory. We cut across Hairsprinkle Park, skipping the bridge and jumping across the little stream. Soymilk used to enjoy all those TV stunts, but now she was cooped up in our little field, doing the same old hurdles over and over again. She was happy to see some real action. We both were.

I saw a couple of weird groups walking around as we rode through town, a bunch of barbers and another bunch of grocery store clerks with aprons and name tags. Either these people had all picked the same Halloween costume and then forgot to take it off, or they were more of Fako's brainwashed gangs, like those awful bodybuilders from the trolley.

When we got near the factory, I slowed Soymilk down. I wanted to scope the place out a bit before I tried to get in. It's like Ol' Gramps always said on my TV show, "Sometimes you gotta use your brains or you'll get your butt kicked."

*I*t was pretty dark by this time. Kind of hard to see, but that might work in my favor, I thought. I was glad I was wearing black.

I was surprised by the number of guards around the Heidelberg factory. They looked like plumbers. Sagging pants, tool belts, plungers . . . and machine guns.

I dismounted Soymilk and left her in an alley. Then I took a lap around the building, keeping as far away from it as I could. There were six plumbers guarding the main gate and four at the big doors the trolley had gone through. These were the only entrances—everywhere else, the building was surrounded by a high metal fence. There were a bunch more plumbers driving around and around the perimeter in golf carts.

"I wonder exactly how high that fence is," I said to myself as I walked back to Soymilk.

"Two point eight five meters," said somebody. "That

would be about nine feet and a few inches to you Americans."

I dropped to the ground, crouching in the darkness and reaching for the throwing knives in my pack.

"Don't be scared," said the voice again. A mean voice with a thick European accent. Not exactly French but sort of French. "It is not to hurt you that I am here. In fact, we seem to be on the same side. We both would enter the Heidelberg factory, but are blocked by the many guards."

A figure emerged from the shadows of the alley. He was one scary-looking nut job, I'll tell you that. He was pushing a bicycle. He carefully leaned it against a Dumpster.

"Why do you want to go in there?" I asked.

"Simply to retrieve what was once mine. What is still a part of me and still belongs to me and only me. That which was born of my blood and shall be returned to me even if it means spilling the blood of another. And you?"

"Uh . . . I'm meeting a friend," I said.

"A friend? In there?" The man's neck got all veiny.

"Yes, but he's not one of them," I said quickly. "He's a prisoner of them."

"Ah," sighed the man. "Then we are on the same side

after all. But I fear we are outnumbered. The guards are many, and the fence is high. It's brand-new, by the way. You can tell it's just been put up. Never rained upon. It's an effective deterrent. There is no time to climb over it, because of those golf carts going around and around. I fear I must wait until I will have made better . . . uh . . ."

"Preparations?" I suggested.

"Yes," he muttered. "Yes, I fear it is impossible to get in tonight."

"For you, maybe," I said, standing up and giving Soymilk two quick pats on the shoulder, "but not for a cowgirl."

Two pats was the code for our famous Brazilian Running Mount. In a flash I was on Soymilk's back and we were out of the alley and galloping toward the fence.

As we got near the fence, one of the golf carts appeared around the corner. I heard shouts.

"They're after us! C'mon, Soymilk!"

We turned hard, Soymilk hugging the fence corner like she used to do in our rodeo barrel races. We galloped along next to the fence. I looked back and saw the golf cart closing on us fast. One plumber was driving, and the other was waving his gun. I doubted he could hit me, but Soymilk was a big target.

Time to get over that fence. Time for some trick riding.

I got to my knees and started to stand up. Soymilk stumbled, probably on some uneven pavement. I almost fell off, but I grabbed on to her mane. She hates that, but she probably understood.

I looked back. The golf cart hadn't gained on us much; Soymilk is hard to beat.

We were coming to another fence corner. A second

golf cart came skidding around it, heading right for us. In a second, we'd be caught in the middle.

No more time to waste. I stood up, riding Soymilk's back like a surfboard in a hurricane.

"Now, Soymilk!"

She jumped. Not over the fence, of course, just enough to give me a boost. I was the one who jumped over the fence. Halfway over, I remembered that when we did this stunt on the show I had an air bag to land on.

I looked down. If it was concrete, I was a goner.

It turned out to be some sort of hairy mass. I landed on it, nice and soft . . . soft but hairy. It felt kind of like a big pile of wigs.

From the other side of the fence I heard the plumbers shouting and Soymilk's hoofbeats racing into the night. Good, she had gotten away. It was a relief to know she'd be out there, waiting and listening in case I whistled for help.

I tried to clamber out of the tangly pile of stuff I had landed in. I realized it *was* a big pile of wigs. I saw a tag on one of them: OFFICIAL JODIE O'RODEO NOVELTY WIG. They were right next to the Dumpsters.

Getting into the building was easy-peasy. There were big double doors nearby that they must use for hauling out trash and unsold merchandise, like my wigs.

DO NOT PROP OPEN said a big sign on one of the doors, which was propped open with a brick. I just walked in. There was a freight elevator right there. So I got in. Pushed four, which was the highest number, and up I went.

About halfway up, I heard alarms going off. Great, everybody in the whole building was going to be looking for me now.

I took off my backpack and got out some of my stuff in case there was trouble. To tell you the truth, I was going to be disappointed if there wasn't at least a little trouble. I tucked a knife in each boot and slung the lasso over my shoulder.

The elevator doors opened at the top floor.

I took a careful peek out into a long hallway. Nobody there! Maybe everybody had run downstairs to look for me.

I raced down the hallway, glancing at the doors.

WHOOPEE CUSHION TESTING DEPARTMENT.

VOTING MACHINE RIGGING DEPARTMENT.

FAKO MUSTACHO, CEO. PRIVATE. KEEP OUT.

CLEARANCE LEVEL ZED ALPHA ONLY.

The CEO's office! I tapped on the door.

"Lenny? Are you in there?"

"Yes! I can't believe you came! Look down."

I looked down and saw a key being pushed under the door.

I bent down and grabbed it. It all seemed so easy.

As I put the key in the lock, I wondered what we would do when we saw each other. Hug? Kiss? On the lips?

I turned the knob, and the door was yanked open from the other side.

There was a wolfman standing there.

"Jodie! You came! I don't believe it!" said the wolfman.

It was Lenny. Thank greasy goodness he's not still dressed like me, I thought. He was a werewolf now. A really cute werewolf!

I put out my arms. He put out his. We were stepping toward each other . . .

"Oh no!" he groaned. "I guess you didn't get my second e-mail about your hat!"

He grabbed my hat and threw it on the ground and stomped on it. This ticked me off big-time.

"What in the name of Hardee's is your problem with my hat?"

"It was bugged, Miss O'Rodeo," said someone behind me.

I turned and saw a mime coming down the hall with a smart-aleck grin on his white face. Behind him were five guys in white karate outfits.

"Oh, yes," said the mime. "The camera in your hat made it easy for us to follow your little plan. We watched you pick out your little jacket, and we saw your little horse ride. Nice jumping. We've had plenty of time to get ready for your little rescue mission. Now, please, step into the boss's office with your little boyfriend."

"Wait," said Lenny. "She only came to give me some food. She's not part of this. Just let her go and I'll go back in the office."

"OK," said the mime. "It's a deal."

You know what I thought about that? I thought, What would be the point? What would I do if they let me go? Go back home and sit around watching *Elmo's World* with the twins? Not that I have anything against Elmo, but how could I enjoy anything when all this was unsolved? When Lenny was still in trouble?

Then I remembered Ol' Gramps and his "Use your brain first" line. But you know what? Gramps was a pain in the neck and a bad actor too.

"No thanks," I told the mime. "You clowns can either let us both go or get your heinies kicked. What'll it be?"

"First of all, I'm not a clown. I'm a mime. Second of all, do you really think you can kick the heinies of Hairsprinkle's top ten karate instructors?"

"I only see five."

"Look behind you."

Yep, the other five were back there. We were surrounded.

I reached for my guns. I'm a pretty quick draw. I had them pointing in the mime's face before he could blink.

"Sorry, Miss O'Rodeo, but we know they're water pistols," sneered the mime. "We saw you filling them up earlier. There was a camera in your hat, remember?" His face paint made his smirk just too ding-dang much to take.

I squirted him good. Right in the eyes!

His face paint started to run.

"NOOOOO! It stings!!!! This face paint is a known eye irritant! I've got to go rinse and repeat until it's all out!" screamed the mime. "Karate instructors, ATTACK!"

They started to close in, slowly, doing that sort of crab-style walk they do.

"Wow," said Lenny, stepping out of the office to stand next to me. "You are one amazing cowgirl!"

"Thanks," I said, "and you're a pretty awesome . . . uh . . . werewolf guy."

We looked each other in the eye. And I knew—and I think he knew—that we were in love.

I leaned in to kiss him. One sweet kiss before we got clobbered.

"Careful," he said, "my nose is loaded."

Good grief.

I stepped back to take a look. His nose did look pretty jacked up.

He stuck a finger into one nostril, turned toward the closest karate instructor, and snorted. *Fizz!* A slimy blob of snot flew out and hit the guy right in the face. Karate guy tried to brush it away, and soon he was entangled in putrid green snot.

I watched in amazement as Lenny put his finger into the other nostril, but I was grabbed from behind before I saw what happened next.

I had one arm free, so I dropped a pistol and grabbed for one of my knives. I swung it wildly behind me. The karate instructor dodged it easily, but he had to let go of me a little and I slipped loose.

I couldn't imagine actually stabbing someone with

a knife, so I gave it an extra half flip when I threw it. It hit the guy handle-first right between the eyes. He stumbled back, and now I had room to swing the lasso.

After that things were pretty crazy.

Once I had roped a couple of guys and hit another one with my other knife, I didn't have anything left to fight with. I glanced at Lenny. He was shocking the bojangles out of a guy with what appeared to be a pack of gum. But it must have run out of juice, because I saw him throw it down.

There were four karate guys still standing, and they were closing in on us. We were back to back, and I was getting ready for a bare-knuckled brawl.

Then the doors burst open at the end of the hall. It was our old friends the bodybuilders, followed by an angry mob of craft-store employees.

"I've got one thing left that might give us a couple of seconds," whispered Lenny. "Get ready to jump for that blue door over there."

He pulled out a grenade and held it up.

"OK, fools! Prepare to die!" he screamed. The brain-washed henchmen and henchwomen stopped running. Some started to back away.

We shuffled toward the blue door.

Lenny pulled the pin and dropped the grenade.

Everybody fell to the floor and covered their heads. Except us. We ran through the door, which I just had time to notice said CATWALK.

I stepped out into nothingness. A vast empty space, with the floor miles below. But I wasn't falling. I felt like Wile E. Coyote, waiting to fall. But I still didn't.

Then I realized there was a steel grid under our feet. You could see right through it, all the way to the floor far below.

Lenny slammed the door shut. I was bracing for an explosion.

"HOO-HOO-HA-HA-HOO-HOO-HA-HA-HA!" Insane laughter was coming from the other side. Were those goons laughing at us?

"It was Heidelberg's LaughBomb!" shouted Lenny above the hoo-hoo-ha-ha. "Try to hold the door shut while I see if one of these keys fits."

The laughter must have had a paralyzing effect on the karate instructors and the rest, because Lenny had plenty of time to find the right key and lock the door before anyone even tried to open it.

We ran across the catwalk. Under our feet—four stories down—was the Heidelberg factory floor. It was huge and kind of noisy. Some of the machines were still running.

There were big stamper machines that would slam together and then open up and a couple of Spock ears or something would slide down a little chute. Another machine had giant spools of blue hair and was spitting out curly blue wigs that look just like the wigs that girl wears on the show that replaced mine, *Bobby and Blu*, starring Roxy Diamond. Goshamighty, I hate her.

Just a few feet below us, a big vat of green snot-like goo was slowly chugging around and around until the goo came out of a big metal chute on the side and went zigzagging off through the factory like a totally unclean waterslide. Conveyor belts were carrying big empty boxes that would stop under a machine and get filled up with glittery confetti.

I wish I could have seen more, but there was no time. The banging on the door behind us was intense. They must have been karate chopping it with their bare hands!

"They'll be through that door in seconds!" I called to Lenny.

"Look down there," he said, pointing at the floor. "I see an exit sign. We just need to get down the ladder and make a run for it."

"What ladder?" I asked.

*I*f you were standing on a catwalk that you really needed to get off of fast and you didn't have a ladder but you did have a big vat of liquid boogers right under you, you would think of the same solution.

Lenny and I realized it at the same time. We both pointed, looked at each other, nodded, and jumped.

At the last second, I started to worry that it was going to be hot. Maybe the vat was a goo cooker.

It wasn't hot. But it was way weird. I hit the surface hard and kept going down. It was like diving in a pool, except instead of a splash it made a big burping sound as it sucked us under.

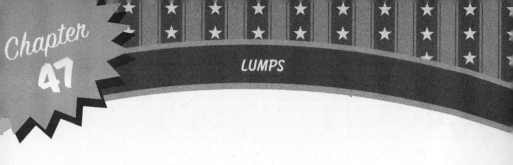

I realized I was in big trouble. I was under goo and I hadn't taken all that big of a breath before I jumped.

It was so thick and it just surrounded me and seemed to be squeezing tighter and tighter. And when I tried to move my arms to swim, it was like there was nothing there to push against.

Then I felt a strong suction pulling me, and I got sucked out of the vat and into a chute that became a trough for the river of goo. Gasping for breath, I pawed at the snot covering my eyes, then looked for Lenny.

I saw him right behind me, all coated in green snot. He must have swallowed some of the goo, because he was snorting it out of his nose! It was the most disgusting thing I'd seen since . . . well, since he used that weird booger blaster a few minutes earlier. I looked away.

That's when I realized we were moving—very, very

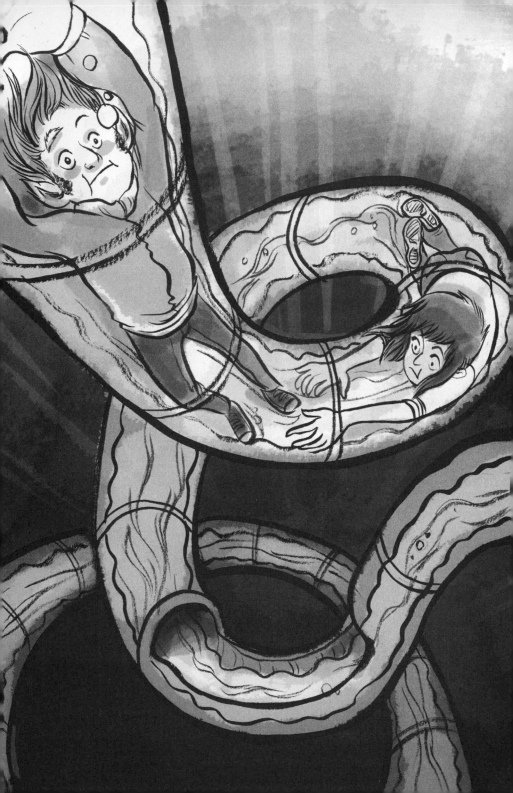

slowly. It really was like one of those water slides at Six Flags Over Hairsprinkle. Just a lot slower.

"Lenny! We're—" I started. But then I heard the sound I had been dreading: The catwalk door banged open, and the karate instructors and bodybuilders came stomping out onto the catwalk, yelling and hollering.

We lay as flat as we could in the goo trough. I hoped that from above we would look like nothing more than two lumpy boogers in the stream of snot.

"They got down somehow!" shouted somebody, probably that cruddy mime. "Everybody downstairs! We got a werewolf and a rodeo queen on the loose. Search the factory! Cover every exit! Shoot to kill! And somebody leave a note for the goo department. Looks pretty lumpy tonight."

*T*here was nothing to do but just lie there and slowly, slowly ooze down the trough to get to wherever it was we were going.

What I could see, by looking past my feet, was the goo-bottling machine about twenty feet away. At some point, the trough would drip us out down there, and we were going to be too lumpy to go any farther.

The karate guys must have given up on the catwalk and come down in the elevator. I could hear them searching the factory below us. Then the mime came in and started shouting at them.

"All right—the plumbers say they haven't gotten out. That means they're in the building somewhere. We're going to search till we find them. Harris, you and MacKenzie stay here and guard the door. The rest of you, split up and check every hallway and . . ."

The voice faded and I figured they were too far away to hear us, but I whispered anyway.

"Hey, Lenny. Are you OK?"

"Yeah. How about you?"

"Fine. But we're going to come to the end of the trough before too long. We can't stay here."

"What do you think?" whispered Lenny. "Should we try fighting our way past Harris and MacKenzie?"

"I've got another idea," I whispered back.

And I told him about what I could see up ahead.

In a minute, the trough was going to pass over a conveyor belt. Every few seconds, a big dishwasher-size box came riding along on the belt on its way to a machine that filled it full of confetti or something. Then the conveyor belt went through a door in the wall to who knows where.

"If we time it right, we can hop right into a box."

"Sounds good to me," he said. "You've done a great job so far."

"Are you making fun of me?" I asked, since after all, I had almost gotten him killed and then made him jump into a vat of fake snot.

"No, I'm serious. You saved my life, I think. And I'm not even sure why."

"Because I like you."

"Oh! You mean you—"

"Shhh! Here comes a box. I'm going for it."

I didn't jump into the box so much as drip into it. The goo made it a slow-motion sort of thing, which was good, because that way I only made a little plop when I landed.

A few seconds later, I heard another little plop that must have been Lenny getting into a box.

I wished I had something to poke a hole in the box with. Then I remembered the fence-mending tool. It was tough getting it out of the backpack, but it easily made a hole big enough to peek out of with one eye. You know, a fence-mending tool really is an incredibly useful thing to have.

I put my eye against the hole and looked out, just in time to see I was about to go under the confetti machine. Like a total idiot, I looked up . . . and got whammed right in the face by about twenty pounds' worth of tiny pieces of paper!

Then another machine closed the lid and taped it shut.

For a second, I thought I was going to suffocate. I was buried under a kamillion bits of paper! Then I remembered I could put my mouth to the hole and breathe. I wondered if Lenny had had time to make a hole.

I squirmed around a little bit so I would have enough room to take a breath and then looked back through the hole.

I could see where the conveyor belt was about to go through the wall. Instead of a door, there were strips of thin plastic hanging down. The box pushed them aside, and suddenly I was in a totally different room.

I could hear people talking and shouting orders. Not like the mime or the brainwashed karate guys. I got a look at a couple of them, and they looked like regular factory workers.

"All right, Linda," I heard a voice say from nearby. "There's the last two boxes for this truck."

Suddenly, I felt myself being picked up.

"Jiminy H. Cricket, this stuff is heavy!" said a woman's voice.

It must be Linda, I realized.

"Yes, it's heavy," said the first voice. "But it's an honor to carry it, isn't it?"

"Yeah, it's an honor," said Linda, "but it's killing my cockamamy back!"

And then I got slammed down hard. And then another box got slammed down hard right next to me.

I could see a hole in that box! And an eyeball looking out! It was Lenny! He waved a goo-covered finger at me; it had little bits of red, white, and blue confetti stuck to it. I waved back with my own confetti-covered finger.

"All right," someone shouted. "This load's ready to go."

Then a door slammed, and it got totally dark.

An engine rumbled. The box slid a little bit as we started moving.

We were stuck in boxes, covered in goo and confetti, in the dark, in the back of a truck, going to who knew where.

I had to wonder: Had I saved Lenny or just gotten us in worse trouble?

S o there I am in the box in the truck trying to hide, and my cell phone goes off. The ringtone was the theme from my show, which was kind of embarrassing.

Anyway, I grabbed it as fast as I could and turned the ringer off. It said I had a text message.

SORRY I MISSD UR 2ND VISIT 2 FACTORY.
CAN I MKE IT UP 2 U W/ DINNR & A MOVIE?
MAYBE @ WHITE HOUSE ON WED? AM
ALMOST PRESIDENT U KNOW. U COULD B
THE 1ST GRLFRND! ROK THE VOTE! FAKO

*A*re you OK, Lenny?" I whispered.

"Yeah," he said. "Are you?"

"Yeah. I wonder where we're going."

"My guess is Hairsprinkle Municipal Stadium," he said.

"What? How could you possibly know that."

"When I was stuck in Fako's office, I read through his plans. He's going to have a big victory party at the stadium after he wins the election."

"He must be pretty sure he's going to win."

"Yeah. I'm pretty sure he'll win too. Not only has he brainwashed most of the country, but if people vote against him, he's got the voting machines rigged anyway. He's practically got it won already. The party is a sure thing."

"Well, the party's over when I get out of this truck," I said. I wished Lenny could have seen the wild look of determination on my face.

That's when the truck sort of lurched forward, stopped, and then started backing up. I could tell it was backing up because it was going *beep, beep, beep*.

"A little more!" we heard someone yelling. "A little more! Hold it! HOLD IT!"

Bump.

"Didn't you hear me yell 'Hold it,' you stupid mime?"

"I'm not a mime, I'm a clown, jerk face! There's a big difference. Now shut your mouth and unload my truck!"

I heard the doors open, and I peeked out of the little hole in the cardboard.

A couple of professional football players started unloading the boxes from our truck. I don't watch football, because I don't like contact sports—except for bull riding. But I recognized one of them from a toilet paper commercial and the other from the news.

Toilet paper guy picked up Lenny's box!

"Gee, this box is heavy!" said toilet paper guy.

"Look," said the other one. "I can pick up five of these boxes at once!"

Unfortunately, I was the fifth box, stacked way up on top. The guy was strong, but he wasn't very good at balancing stuff. He dropped my box! Ding-dang, dude, could you be a little more careful?

My box hit the floor hard, but the confetti cushioned me. The top burst open.

I'm done for, I thought. I clenched my fists—that football player might be able to overpower me, but I wasn't going to make it easy on him.

But then somebody just closed the box back up and patted the tape back down.

I got picked up again, carried a little ways, and then put down. I heard footsteps walking away and coming back. More boxes being put down. And finally I heard a door closing.

H ey, Jodie, are you in here? Everybody's gone now."
We both clambered out of our boxes and looked
around.

Lenny looked absolutely awful—completely coated
in confetti that had stuck to the goo. I looked down
and saw that I was too. I held up my hand, and for the
first time I saw that the confetti was stamped with
teeny gold letters: CONGRATULATIONS, PRESIDENT FAKO!
TODAY THE UNITED STATES, TOMORROW THE WORLD!

We were in a pretty huge room, heaped with messy
piles of boxes. I guess brainwashed football players
aren't big on neatness.

"We're locked in," said Lenny, going over to the
door and rattling the handle. "It's a dead bolt. This
must be where they store supplies and stuff during
the football season. Maybe there are some nachos in
here somewhere! I'm starving."

"If not, I do have some Pop-Tarts for you," I said,

pointing to my crushed, mangled, goo-covered backpack.

"Uh, thanks, but let's look around first," he said.

We found more boxes full of confetti. And some boxes with PRESIDENT FAKO! T-shirts and baseball caps and buttons and temporary tattoos and pom-poms. All of it had been made by the Heidelberg Novelty Company.

Thankfully, there was also some bottled water with Fako's picture on the label. They said "H_2FakO." But no nachos or other food. That must be stored in the stadium's snack bars, I guess.

We sat down next to each other on a box and drank some water and ate some smushed Pop-Tarts. Lenny pulled a bag of pork rinds out of the pocket of his wolfman sweater.

"I also have an edible eraser shaped like a chicken," he said, "but let's save that as a last resort."

Then we both just sat there quietly for minute.

"Are you thinking what I'm thinking?" I asked.

"What are you thinking?" he asked, and he turned to look at me and our shoulders touched and we were so close and he had a look on his confetti-speckled face like he wanted to kiss me.

But I really, really, *really* had to say what I had been thinking: "How are we going to go to the bathroom?"

"Oh," said Lenny.

Well, I know it was bad timing, but who wants to have their first kiss at the same time their bladder is exploding?

"I guess we could take turns going behind some of those boxes over there," said Lenny.

"OK," I said. "I have GOT to go first. Don't look and don't listen."

I went behind the biggest pile and looked for a good place to go.

"That wasn't too bad," I said when I got back. "I peed on a bunch of I ♥ FAKO sweatpants."

"Oh, man! I needed some ungooey pants!"

"Sorry, too late now," I said.

That about did it for the romance, I guess.

We found a dry box of Fako sweatpants and some T-shirts with a picture of Fako's head on Mount Rushmore. We also found a box of Fako rally towels, so we were able to strip down and wipe the goo off ourselves (while hiding behind boxes, of course) before putting the new stuff on.

It felt great to get out of my slimy clothes, but I felt a little bit weird about Lenny seeing me without my cowgirl stuff on. Lenny had destroyed my hat back at the factory and now I had on an ugly T-shirt instead of my cool black cat jacket, and sweatpants instead of my real cowgirl riding clothes. Without all that stuff, I look just like a regular girl. I wasn't sure if he'd still like me.

But then I had the surprise of seeing *him* without a cowgirl outfit or a werewolf costume for the first time. I had been right. He was really cute. A little nerdier than I had realized, but still cute.

We just looked at each other for a minute.

"I guess we better start figuring out how to get out of here and save the world, huh?" I said.

"Yeah, I guess so," he said.

After about thirty seconds of messing with the door, we realized we'd never get out that way.

"We're locked in until someone opens the door in the morning," I said.

"And then that person will see us and lock the door on us again."

"We need a great plan!"

Half an hour later, when we gave up trying to think of a plan, we just started talking. I mean really talking. First it was just about our lives and our families, and then it was secret stuff. The kind of stuff you don't tell anybody—except the right person.

At one point, I was telling Lenny some stuff about being in Hollywood, when I remembered *The A-Team*.

"Hey, you remember the guy on my show named Mr. Wallaby?"

"You mean the Australian ghost who use to say 'Boooo, mate'?"

"Right. Anyway, a long time ago he was on this show called *The A-Team*. Not the movie, the TV show. And he told me once that in every episode they would get locked in a garage by the bad guys and they would use the stuff in the garage to make like a trash-can tank or an old dishwasher that shot out flaming pickles or something. And when the bad guys came back—*kablammo!*"

"Why were there pickles in a garage and how did they light them on fire?" asked Lenny.

"I have no idea. But the thing is, they used stuff that the bad guys didn't realize would be dangerous. Maybe there's something like that in here."

We rooted around in the boxes some more looking for flammable pickles or whatever.

The best thing we came up with was putting the water bottles in with the confetti. Maybe when they dropped the confetti, one of the water bottles would hit Fako on the head.

"I'm so tired, I can't tell if that's a good idea or not," Lenny said. "I've been up forever. I've got to get some sleep."

"Yeah, that's a good idea."

Earlier, I think we would have been bashful about the sleeping arrangements, but now we were both so tired that we just piled up some confetti into beds and went to sleep.

I was having another one of my dreams where I'm back on the set in Hollywood. It's weird because the other actors are never the real actors from the show and we never seem to get around to actually filming anything. And then just when we're about to start, I wake up.

"Rise, shine, and save the world," Lenny said. "I've heard some people going by outside. Nobody has tried the door yet, but somebody could open it at any second. We'd better get ready. And we've GOT to think of a plan. We've only got twenty-four hours until Election Day."

"Don't you think maybe somebody else has stopped him by now?" I said. "Maybe the CIA or something."

"Maybe, but I doubt it. I wish we knew what was going on out there."

"Don't you still have your cell phone?"

"Yeah, but there's nobody to call."

"I know, but can't you check the news, weather, and horoscopes and stuff like that on it?"

When the first headline came up, we both gasped in horror:

ELECTION DAY CHANGED TO MONDAY

"Why wait till Tuesday?" said the frontrunner, Governor Fako Mustacho.

His top opponents have both agreed to the unprecedented change.

"I can't wait to vote for Fako," said Republican candidate Rhonda Horvath.

"Me neither, dude," said Democratic candidate William G. Murray. "He rocks! I'm his biggest fan evah!"

"No way, stoopid! I am his biggest fan evaaaah," responded Horvath. "Check out the 'Vote Fako' temporary tattoo on my forehead."

"That's nothing," replied Murray, pointing to his own forehead. "My tattoo's permanent!"

Polls open at 7 A.M. Massive voter turnout is expected.

"What time is it now?" Lenny asked.

I pointed to the time display on his cell phone: 7:12 A.M.

"So much for our twenty-four hours," he said. "We're already twelve minutes late."

"True," I said, "but now I've got a plan."

*P*ut on one of every Fako thing you can find," I said. "WE are going to be his biggest fans 'evah.' When someone opens this door, we start cheering and yelling 'Hooray Fako!' and we'll just tell them we wanted to get here early to get good seats."

"Wow, Jodie, you are one amazing cowgirl!" said Lenny, and I blushed like crazy.

We started piling the stuff on, especially stuff that would help hide our faces, like Fako hoodies and sunglasses. Then we covered ourselves with buttons and stickers and stuff. We picked up some red, white, and blue Fako pom-poms and waited by the door, ready to start cheering when it opened.

It didn't open.

We sat down but stayed ready. It still didn't open.

We started to get really hungry. We had eaten all the Pop-Tarts and pork rinds the night before, so we shared the edible chicken-shaped eraser. It was delicious!

Absolutely amazing. Lenny said that after this was all over, he was going to see if he could buy some more at Sven's Fair Price Store.

Finally, we heard footsteps. They stopped at the door. The lock clicked. The door opened, and there were the two football players who had unloaded us the day before.

"Who the heck are you?" said the box-dropper.

"I'm Fako's biggest fan!" I yelled, jumping up and shaking the pom-poms, being careful to keep them in front of my face.

"No!" yelled Lenny. "I'm his biggest fan! Whoo!"

"No, me! Squeee!" we hollered, dancing around the men.

"Yay!" yelled Lenny. "We're excited about politics and the democratic process!"

"I hate cheerleaders," said the box-dropper. "They never pay any attention to the game, they just shout and giggle."

"Really?" said toilet paper guy. "I've always found their positive energy to be *positively* contagious!"

"Thanks!" I said. "Do you know where we can get in line? We want front-row seats!"

"Yeah," said Lenny. "And we want to get our picture taken with Fako. Do you know where he is?"

"I heard he's using our locker rooms down on the lower level. Try there," said toilet paper guy. "But he's going to be giving his victory speech soon, so you'd better hurry."

"Victory speech?" Lenny said, sounding a lot less like a fan. "It's only ten thirty in the morning."

"Well, that's what the TV says," said toilet paper guy, pointing to a screen mounted on the wall nearby.

"Great, we'll go take a look! Yay, Fako!"

"Yippee," said Lenny, sounding like a very depressed cheerleader.

We squeezed past the football players and were out of the storeroom at last. But we weren't free yet, and we still had no way of stopping Fako. A crowd was standing around the TV, watching *Good Morning Hairsprinkle*.

"Let's take a look at our 3-D, holographic, artificially intelligent electoral map, Jim."

"Do we have to, Nancy? The 3-D holographs give me a headache."

"Yes, Jim, we must. It shows that Fako Mustacho has received one hundred percent of the vote in all the states that have reported in so far. Thanks to another brilliant idea of Fako Mustacho's, the polls will be closing in about half an hour. After that we'll be able to officially call the race in Fako Mustacho's favor and then go have lunch."

"Truly an amazing story, Nancy. Just a few weeks ago no one had even heard of Fako Mustacho, and we all thought that a Republican or a Democrat would win."

"Yes, Jim, we were fools back then. We, the people, have seen the light. Our polls report that one hundred percent of voters say that the minute they saw Mustacho for the first time, they knew that he and his mustache were right for our country."

"It really seems like a shame that we'll have to wait until Inauguration Day for Fako to become our supreme leader, Nancy."

"Jim, sources close to Capitol Hill tell me that Congress may make an emergency amendment to the Constitution so that Fako Mustacho could become president as early as next week."

"And not a moment too soon!"

"Hooray," said the crowd in unison. "Let's start selling some souvenirs!"

They all rushed into our storeroom, grabbed boxes, and ran down the hall to a souvenir stand, where hundreds of people were lined up to buy Fako stuff.

"Man, look at all those people," I said.

"If we go out there, we'll never get near him," said Lenny.

"Let's try another door."

O K, I'm not going to bore you by telling you about every lousy hallway and storeroom that we ran through and every stairway we went up and down. There were a lot. If they make this into a movie, they can just have a music montage of us running around really fast. We had one of those on just about every episode of my show.

Then we saw a sign that said LOCKER ROOM.

There were a bunch of guys in black suits standing around the door. Secret Service agents!

"This must be it!" I whispered.

"Let's go for it!"

"Please! Please let us see Fako! We just want a picture, please, dude! Let us in! Just for a second? Please . . ."

"Sure, go on in, kids," said an agent, and he opened the door for us.

Holding our big #1 fingers in front of our faces, we walked in. We had made it!

Now all we had to do was grab the mustache and the whole thing would be over.

Then Fako turned toward us and smiled.

"Ah, Lenny Junior! And Miss O'Rodeo! What a pleasure it is to see you again! Especially you, Jodie."

He was on to us.

"Go!" shouted Lenny.

We lunged for the mustache.

The Secret Service agents grabbed us before we even got close.

"You—" I shouted before someone put his hand over my mouth.

Fako walked over and whispered to us, "These guys are the real thing. Not even brainwashed. Just doing their job. Be careful."

As he whispered, the mustache was so close to me it was almost tickling my ear.

I tried to get a hand free to grab it. But I couldn't.

"Oh, guys, we've got so much to talk about," Fako said. "But could I trouble you to wait just a second?"

We all stood there and waited.

Then came a roar! A tremendous noise from way over our heads. Coming through layers and layers of concrete. A yelling and a stomping that went on for three or four minutes. Then it was gradually replaced by "FAKO FAKO FAKO FAKO . . ."

"Well, that's that," said Fako. "The TV just announced the closing of the polls. I'm the next president of the U.S. of A."

He sat down in a folding chair and seemed to be thinking about things.

"Oh, I'm sorry, guys. I didn't mean to leave you there like that. Guards, I think you can let these kids go. I think they understand that if they try to attack the duly elected president elect, you will shoot to kill. And that if they say too many bad things about me, I'll have them tried for treason."

The guards let us go.

I made a move for Fako, but two Secret Service agents right behind him leveled their guns at me.

"What are you thinking, Miss O'Rodeo?" said Fako. "These Secret Service guys will shoot you. And I don't want that. I want to be friends again . . . Maybe more than friends with you, Jodie."

"Forget it!" Lenny and I both shouted.

"That's hurtful. Listen, are you still hung up about the mustache? We're past that now. There's been an election. The people have voted."

"You stole their votes!" I shouted.

"Don't you get it?" Lenny yelled at the Secret Service guys. "He stole the election. He cheated."

Fako sighed. One of those sighs that adults make when they think kids are too stupid to explain something to.

"These officers aren't the Federal Election Commission," he said, with a smirk that showed he thought he was being funny. "Look, guys, game over. You got some points here and there, but I won. It's over. It's history. I mean, it's literally going to be in the history books. I won. I'm in charge now.

"All I have to do is say the word and the CIA ships you off to Brownwater Base in Antarctica with all the other wackos who are a danger to this fine country.

"But I don't want to do that. I'm going to give you another option . . . Just admit that it's over. Admit that I'm the new president. And then I'll let you walk out the door."

Lenny and I looked at each other. What could we do?

"I'll go up there and make my speech and I'll tell everyone that you're not the Evil One, Lenny. And I'll tell them that Jodie O'Rodeo has been cleared of all suspicion. No one will ever bother you again."

Lenny opened his mouth to say something, but Fako cut him off.

"Jodie, Lenny . . . remember. I can't tolerate treason or threats against our democratic process. If you say anything other than 'OK, Mr. President,' you'll both be silenced and taken away and that will be it."

"OK," we both grunted.

"OK, *Mr. President*," Fako insisted.

"OK, Mr. President," we mumbled.

PART III

*H*i, it's me, Lenny Jr. again. Here to tell you the rest of the story.

The streets were jammed with cars, and the sidewalks were full of people headed to the stadium. They were all rushing to hear Fako's victory speech.

Everyone but us was yelling and hollering. Everyone but us was happy.

We didn't say anything. We just kept walking.

We were hardly even paying attention to where we were heading. I didn't even know where I was going to go. Home? Yeah, I thought, I guess it's finally safe to go home without my parents wanting to have me arrested.

Then I had this odd thought. If I go home, I'll have to go back to school. And if I go back to school, my best friend won't be there anymore. Weird.

We passed a bench at a bus stop and I sat down. Jodie sat down next to me and put her arm around me. She leaned over and was about to whisper something.

I jumped up and yelled: "That guy's riding my bicycle!!!"

"What?"

"That guy there! He's riding my bicycle! Hey, dude! That's my bike!"

The guy stopped. I saw now that he was the guy I had seen at Sven's way back when. The nut with a wispy mustache . . . and a huge rifle. Well, he didn't have the rifle at Sven's, but he had it now. I really wished I hadn't yelled at him.

"Oh, hey . . . person!" he said in a European accent. Not exactly French but sort of French. "Oh, hey, cowgirl. Nice to see you again."

He turned back to me. "I am very sorry for taking your bicycle. It was wrong and I am apologizing. I shall return it to you in just a few minutes after I take vengeance upon the person that has stolen my mustache! The blood of my blood and hair of my hair! No election can change that. He must die! He will die! And the mustache shall be mine again! See you later!"

And he rode off toward the stadium, snaking between the gridlocked cars.

"I forgot all about that guy!" said Jodie.

"You know him? Who is he?"

"He's a nut with some kind of obsession with Fako's mustache."

"We've got to stop him!"

"Why?" Jodie asked. "I mean, not that I want anybody to kill anybody, but why should I try to help Fako?"

"Fako's not real. He's Casper—my best friend. At least, before I met you, he was. My only friend. I've got to get back there and warn him."

"How are you going to do that?" Jodie said. "That guy has your bicycle and he's already halfway there. The only way you could beat him would be with—"

"NEIGGHHHH!"

A horse came galloping through the crowd. Right toward us!

"Soymilk!" shouted Jodie, jumping to her feet. And the horse stopped as she threw her arms around its neck. I recognized the horse from Jodie's show!

"Oh, sweetie," said Jodie. "Have you been looking for me all this time?"

"Neighhh!"

"Wow! Lenny, this is Soymilk! And—do you really want to try to save Casper?"

"Yes," I said, although I wasn't sure exactly why. I guess it's hard to give up a friend. Even a friend who's a huge pain in the behind sometimes.

*J*odie jumped up onto Soymilk's back. I had to climb aboard from the back of a bench.

"Hold on," Jodie called over her shoulder.

"Wait—hold on to what?"

"To me, I guess."

"Uh, where?" This was the most embarrassing thing I'd ever said in my life, but I really didn't know what to do. I think Jodie was as embarrassed as I was, because she pretended not to hear me.

"Hey-YO-yo-te-do, Soymilk! Away!"

I held on! I'm still not sure exactly where. Everything became a blur. I really mean a blur. We were moving that fast. Dodging and weaving with Jodie shouting, "Hey, there!" and "Look out!" and "Yee-ha!"

Meanwhile, I was getting jostled around so much I thought either my brains or my behind was going to break. "It's going too fast!" I yelled.

"What is?" Jodie yelled back.

"The horse. It's going too fast!"

Jodie looked back just long enough to glare at me.

"Don't ever—ever!—call Soymilk an it! She is a she!"

"Sorry, Soymilk!"

She didn't reply—she just kept on galloping toward the stadium.

We hadn't walked all that far, so it was a pretty short trip back. Soymilk hurtled over an orange construction fence, and we were in the parking lot, crashing into TV reporters and knocking over lights and stuff.

Then a jump over a concrete barrier and I could see the stadium bouncing around dead ahead.

"Stop! We order you to stop!" someone was shouting.

"Things are about to go nuts," Jodie shouted. "Just lean when I lean."

She leaned and I leaned, and Soymilk seemed to lean too. We seemed to be changing direction, but the back of the horse seemed to be doing it a little differently from the front.

"Other way!" Jodie yelled. And we did it again on the other side.

"Now duck!"

Suddenly, there was a lot of beeping. I looked back and realized we had just bolted through a metal detector. I saw a guard raising his gun, but the crowd was too thick for him to shoot. There were people everywhere, and for a moment we got bogged down.

So Jodie and Soymilk (and me too, I guess) did that Lone Ranger thing. You know, where Silver the horse rears back and waves his front legs in the air. What I didn't realize is that it's very hard to keep from falling off when that happens. But I held on. Again, I can't say exactly to what.

The Lone Ranger thing worked, and the crowd parted for us a little bit and we pushed our way through a big gateway and we were inside the stadium. The noise was insane. The people in the stands must have been screaming their heads off. That probably meant Fako was giving his victory speech, which meant he was an easy target for the sort of French mustache assassin.

"Look!" I yelled to Jodie. There was big orange tape blocking a low hallway that didn't have any people in it.

Soymilk bolted for the tape. Suddenly, a woman in a yellow vest leaped in front of us.

"OK, everyone, we need to clear a path here. Please have your horse clear the path!"

It was the crazy annoying lady from in front of the Chinese restaurant again.

Soymilk tried to stop, but she slipped on the tile floor of the hallway and crashed right into the lady, who went sprawling into a bin of unwashed football jerseys.

Soymilk had cleared a path.

Soymilk got her feet under her again and plunged down the tunnel-like hallway. The hallway was shorter than I thought, and at the end was . . . an escalator.

I still don't know how you ride a horse down an escalator. But we did. It was an up escalator too.

All I know is we hit the bottom and we saw a big opening ahead, with noise and light pouring through.

Then we were out under the lights and surrounded by 132,453 people. We raced across the field, which was real grass, not Astroturf. We came up behind a big stage that had been set up for Fako's speech. It was surrounded by TV equipment trucks and, unfortunately, about twenty-five Secret Service agents.

"There's an assassin in the stadium!" I yelled. "A sort of French guy! With my bike and a big gun!"

But they weren't listening to me. They were drawing their own guns.

We were too fast for them, though. Jodie and I leaned and Soymilk turned in a split second, just like the champion rodeo horse she used to be. Soymilk jumped over a huge tangle of cords.

And—hey, wait, was that my bike propped up against an equipment truck?

We leaned again as Soymilk rounded the back of the truck and burst into an area of dozens of anchorpeople all saying: "And now let's go live to Fako Mustacho's victory speech."

We zigged and zagged between them, bumping a few along the way.

Up ahead, several Secret Service agents were waiting for a chance to shoot us without hitting an anchorperson. But Jodie was pointing.

"There he is!" she screamed, and at first I thought she meant Fako, who was standing on the stage with his arms outstretched. But then I saw the sort of French guy standing at the front of the crowd, aiming his rifle at Fako.

I don't know what the Secret Service agents did next. I hardly even know what Jodie did next. I let go with one hand to grab the very last thing I had to fight with: the Ultra-Sticky-Stretchy Grabber Hand.

Unfortunately, that's when Soymilk made a leap for the stage. I lost my grip with my other hand.

I could feel myself falling.

In two seconds everything was over.

*I*f we were watching it in slow motion, here's what happened in that two seconds:

I have a glimpse of Fako standing on the stage with his arms raised. Confetti and water bottles are falling from somewhere up above.

As Soymilk's front hooves hit the stage, I lose my hold and start to fall. Soymilk just seems to move out from under me, and Jodie urges her forward toward the sort of French guy, who is squeezing the trigger.

In my right hand is the Ultra-Sticky-Stretchy Grabber Hand. Even as I'm falling and putting my left hand out to break my fall, my right arm is in motion. My wrist is flicking, my index finger is tightening its grip on the long stringy part, and my thumb is loosening its hold on the hand.

BANG! The sort of French guy's gun goes off.

And *ZZZZZZTTTTT*, I whip the sticky hand out like lightning. It flies out and out—not toward the gun but toward an invisible point in space where it meets the bullet with a soft, sticky *thwack*.

I'm landing on the stage. The side of my head hits the floor—hard. But I'm yanking back on the sticky hand. It's pulling on the bullet, but the bullet is strong and mean and keeps going.

There's Fako looking a lot like Casper. Scared. Too scared to move or duck or even put his hands down. It's happening too fast for him.

The bullet races on. But the sticky hand is slowing it down. It's been stretched too far. It's pulling back now with amazing strength. Of course, any normal sticky hand would just snap in two. Even a deluxe sticky hand would break. But not this. This is Hank Heidelberg's masterpiece!

The bullet gets closer and closer to Fako, and the hand pulls harder and harder. I'm holding on as tight as I can.

The bullet has lost most of its speed now. It's no longer a killer. But it hasn't spent the last of its energy yet. Just another inch. Another centimeter. Another micron. And it hits Fako. Right in the mustache.

Fako falls backward. The sticky hand snaps back at me so hard that it shatters the bones in my hand.

Before the pain hits me, I look down and see, attached to the sticky hand, the bullet and the mustache.

With my good hand, I grab the mustache, put it between my teeth, and rip it in two. Then I swallow it, and the twirly handlebar parts go down my throat like nasty lukewarm hairy noodles.

The mustache is dead.

Then a water bottle falls on my head and knocks me out.

Chapter 62

*T*hat's the slow-motion replay as I see it in my head. The one they show on TV is a lot different. I'm sure you saw it. They showed it a million times on every channel.

But in case you forgot, here's what it looks like:

We see Fako with his arms up and his mustache looking perfect. Confetti and water bottles are falling all around him. Then the camera jerks wildly and blurrily and zooms in on the right side of the stage.

A sort of French guy is aiming a rifle. Suddenly, a horse appears in the background. You can dimly see a figure falling off the horse, but the TV news anchors say that it's nobody important.

It was me.

The important person is still riding the horse. It's Jodie O' Rodeo—America's teenage rodeo queen and, now, America's heroine.

The sort of French guy's gun fires. Don't worry, viewers, it's just a wild shot. Investigators never even found where the bullet went. But look! Freeze-frame: *He's cocking the gun again! He's going to shoot again, Jim!*

Suddenly, Jodie O'Rodeo is standing on top of the horse!

Just look at her, Nancy, she's standing on the horse!

Now Jodie's leaping off the horse onto the speaker tower and grabbing the sort of French guy. They tumble to the ground. O'Rodeo is grabbing a speaker cord on the way down.

The sort of French guy lands first. Jodie lands with a knee in his back and with one, two, three motions of her arm, hog-ties the would-be assassin.

The camera jerks back to the podium. Fako is gone? What happened? We'll never know.

Every person, including every cameraman and every camerawoman, was watching O'Rodeo take down the assassin. No one saw what happened to Fako. And no one ever saw him again.

The platoon of Secret Service agents and police officers that rushed the stage found only two local Hairsprinkle schoolkids. One with a broken hand and one with a busted lip.

"One of them may have been the figure we saw fall off the horse, but who really cares, Jim?"

"I know I don't care, Nancy, what I want to know is, when will the new season of the Jodie O'Rodeo show start?"

"That's what we all want to know, Jim."

I woke up feeling the strangest sensation. Something warm and soft on my lips.

I opened my eyes.

It was Jodie.

"I wasn't sure you were going to wake up," she said. "So I tried the Sleeping Beauty thing on you. It worked!"

"I'll say!"

I looked around. There were police and official-looking people everywhere. I saw some questioning Casper, who was holding a bloody handkerchief to his mouth.

"His mustache disappeared! They don't realize he's Fako," she whispered in my ear.

"Don't tell them!" I whispered. "They'd lock him up forever."

"They probably should," said Jodie.

"Maybe, but still . . . don't tell. Not yet. And leave me out of it too. We can always tell the full story later."

*A*nd this is later.

In this book, we're finally telling the true story of what happened. Jodie and I wanted the actual truth to be known to historians and scholars someday. But right now it's still top secret. We're going to lock it up in a vault for now. Why change things? They're almost back to normal . . .

"Hey, Lenny," said Sven. "Did you see *The Jodie O'Rodeo National Hero Showdeo* last night?"

"Of course," I said. "I never miss it."

"It's even better than her old show. Can you believe those stunts she's doing? She's amazing!"

"She sure is," I said.

"What are you getting today? A Wet Pets pen, twenty-three edible chicken-shaped erasers, and . . . aw, it's a temporary tattoo of a horse with the words 'Hoofbeats and Heartbeats.' Are you buying this for somebody special?"

"Yeah, I'm going to mail it to . . . er . . . the special somebody."

"Oh, a long-distance love affair," said Sven, actually tearing up. "How sweet."

"Not really," said Casper. "It makes me want to barf."

Sven shot him a nasty look. She rang up my stuff and gave me the tattoo for free. Then Casper paid for his stuff and we went back outside to walk around downtown Hairsprinkle for a while and look at the Christmas decorations.

"C'mon, let's go into Hairsprinkle Hot Dog," said Casper. "My treat."

"First of all," I said, "I'm not letting you treat me to anything until you've given back all the money you stole—"

"Allegedly stole," stuck in Casper. "And anyway, I was going to use the ten dollars that Nana Nookums sent me for Thanksgiving."

"—and second of all," I continued, "it's too hard to eat a big chili dog while I've got this cast on my hand."

"Oh, here we go again with the hand," moaned Casper. "You know I really don't see what you've got to complain about. You got to be on TV, you got to meet a president—"

"A phony president elect," I stuck in.

"—you got your bike back, you got to keep the werewolf costume and the super-powerful sticky hand, *AND* you've got the most beautiful cowgirl in the world writing you love notes from Hollywood all the time. Sounds pretty good to me."

For once, Casper was right. But I wasn't about to say thank you.

"What did you buy at Sven's anyway," I asked him.

"Nothing much . . . ," he said, rolling up a small bag and shoving it in his pocket.

"No—seriously. What was it?"

"Oh, you'll see," he said.

I just hope I don't see it on *Good Morning Hairsprinkle* tomorrow morning.

TOM ANGLEBERGER is the bestselling author of the Origami Yoda series and *Horton Halfpott*. He lives in Virginia and hopes you will visit him online at www.origamiyoda.com.

This book was designed by Meagan Bennett and art directed by Chad W. Beckerman. The illustrations are by Jen Wang. The text is set in 12-point New Century Schoolbook, a typeface derived from Linn Boyd Benton's original 1894 Century Roman.